Please return or renew this item by the last date
shown. There may be a...
so. Items can be retur... ...any Westminster

UNTAMED

 BOOK OF THE FILM

WITHDRAWN

Westminster Libraries

3011780409289 4

Farshore

First published in 2021 in the USA by Little, Brown and Company.
This edition published in Great Britain in 2021 by Farshore

An imprint of HarperCollins*Publishers*
1 London Bridge Street, London SE1 9GF
www.farshore.co.uk

HarperCollins*Publishers*
1st floor, Watermarque Building, Ringsend Road,
Dublin 4, Ireland

Adapted by Claudia Guadalupe Martinez

DreamWorks Spirit Untamed © 2021 DreamWorks Animation LLC.
All Rights Reserved.

ISBN 978 0 7555 0056 7
001
Printed and Bound in the UK using 100% Renewable Electricity at CPI Group (UK) Ltd

A CIP catalogue record for this title is available from the British Library.

All rights reserved. No part of this publication may be reproduced, stored in a retrieval system,
or transmitted in any form or by any means, electronic, mechanical, photocopying,
recording or otherwise, without the prior permission of the publisher and copyright owner.

This book is a work of fiction. Names, characters, places, and incidents are the
product of the author's imagination or are used fictitiously. Any resemblance to
actual events, locales, or persons, living or dead, is coincidental.

DreamWorks Spirit Untamed © 2021 DreamWorks Animation LLC.
All Rights Reserved.

MIX
Paper from
responsible sources
FSC C007454

DreamWorks

Spirit

UNTAMED

 BOOK OF THE FILM

CHAPTER 1

Lucky Prescott looked through old family photographs, lingering on one of her mother that was taken at the Miradero rodeo arena. Her mother, Milagro, true to her name, had been a miracle on a horse. Despite all the years gone by, Lucky still felt sad when she thought about her mother. Lucky flipped to the next photograph. It was her favorite. Her mother and Jim Prescott—Lucky's father—stood by baby Lucky, who sat on a swing in the backyard of their cozy old house. They'd all looked so happy before everything changed.

Lucky put the stack of pictures back on the dresser and sat on the windowsill of her bedroom at the Prescott mansion, where she'd lived with her grandpa and aunt Cora for the past ten years. From atop her perch, Lucky could see guests in fancy attire walking up to the front door of the house. She heard their laughter mingling with the sounds of a band playing. Kids raced toward an ice cream stand, tripping over one another to be first in line.

Lucky wished, more than ever, that she wasn't stuck inside. She felt isolated and lonely.

She swung one of her legs out the window and shelled peanuts, piling them nearby for Bob, her lone friend at the Prescott mansion. Her friend sniffed at the snacks from a distance. "Come on, who's a good squirrel?" she said, holding out a peanut to him. "Come on. They're your favorite." The squirrel approached Lucky's open hand timidly.

"Fortuna Esperanza Navarro Prescott. Lucky! Where are you?" Aunt Cora burst into the room in her party dress. Bob the squirrel scurried away in a panic.

"Oh, Bob!" Lucky said. She drew the curtain closed over herself, trying to hide from Aunt Cora that she was hanging out a window.

"Lucky, proper ladies do not hang out of window ledges," Aunt Cora said. She whipped open the drapes, unimpressed by Lucky's idea of a hiding place. Lucky rolled her eyes and slumped.

"Proper ladies also get to go to *amazing* fun parties," Lucky muttered.

"This is a bit more important than an amazing fun party. Do I need to remind you of what happened at the last event?"

"Mistakes were made."

"Mistakes indeed!" Aunt Cora took a moment to compose herself. "You're not missing anything besides—"

"Cake?" Lucky interrupted. She drew the curtains around her again in frustration and defiance. "Other kids? Fun?"

"Lucky...," Aunt Cora said.

But Lucky did not hear her. All she heard was trumpeting coming from the backyard.

"An *elephant*? Come on!" Lucky could not believe it.

Aunt Cora sighed as she pulled the curtain open again. "I know it's hard to understand. Part of being a Prescott is not always having what you want, but doing what's best for the family," she said.

Lucky whipped the drapes closed again. Aunt Cora whipped them open. Her mouth pursed, and her eyebrows knitted together in disapproval. Lucky could see that Cora was done playing. "Now come down from there and finish your math lesson. If this new tutor of yours has one more nervous breakdown..."

Aunt Cora held out her arm. Lucky took it and Aunt Cora pulled her away from the window ledge. Lucky sat down at her desk and flipped open the math book while

Aunt Cora tidied the room. Lucky sighed. Aunt Cora walked back to her and placed a hand on Lucky's shoulder in a sympathetic gesture.

"If a train traveling twenty-five miles per hour leaves the station at eight AM...," Lucky recited from her book. "Ugh, when will I ever need to know this?"

"Cora? Cora! Show yourself!" Grandpa called from outside the room. He sounded just as determined as Aunt Cora. Before Cora could respond, he rushed into Lucky's room wearing an impeccable black suit and a loose tie. "Cora! This is an emergency!"

Aunt Cora nodded. She reached for the tie around Grandpa's neck and tied it in a neat knot. It was the finishing touch.

"Oh no, too tight!" he exclaimed. "Just think of it: from railroad baron to governor. And why? Because..." He looked at Lucky expectantly. Lucky sighed.

"Prescotts never give up," Lucky and Grandpa said in unison. With that, the adults exited, looking over their shoulders as they did so. Lucky didn't have to wonder why. She could hear them start to whisper just outside her door.

"Are you sure we shouldn't put a lock on that door?" Grandpa asked nervously. The voices faded.

Lucky might as well have been in a cage. She looked out the window again with longing.

Fancy carriages came and went, dropping even more guests off at the front door of the Prescott mansion. Grandpa and Aunt Cora stood at the entrance, looking as formal and poised as ever. They welcomed each of their guests to the Prescott for Governor campaign event.

"Welcome, all! The caviar has been brought in from across the pond," Grandpa bragged.

"You've got my vote," one of their visitors said.

"I'll run the state as firmly as I run my own home," Grandpa said, exuding confidence.

Lucky opened her book and tried to focus on her work. "If a train has to stop every hundred miles to refill water, at what time will the train get to the first water stop?" Lucky mumbled through her math problem. She was interrupted by a slap at the window. She rushed over and threw the curtains open. Bob was back! He jumped inside onto the sill, staring at Lucky and looking sweet.

"Hello, Bob! So nice of you to return, sir," Lucky said.

Suddenly, Bob jumped from the windowsill to Lucky's desk to the dresser. Lucky gasped. He made his way through every surface in the room, knocking over Lucky's books and anything else that got in his way.

"Bob! We talked about this! Bob, you're betraying my trust!" Lucky tried to reason with him, but Bob tore past her and ran up the wall, toward the bedroom door.

With a single push, the door flew open and out ran the squirrel.

Uh-oh, Lucky thought. *Maybe we really should get a lock for that door.*

Lucky rushed after Bob. He ran across the banister lining the landing, and Lucky chased closely behind. She hardly noticed the downstairs ballroom that was beautifully set up for the big event. Her eyes didn't linger on the decorations, the bandstand, the champagne, the cake, or anything else.

"Bob, no. No, come back. Come on, Bob!" Lucky yelled.

But Bob did not stop. The squirrel dodged Lucky and scampered over to a pulley holding Grandpa's official campaign portrait.

"Aunt Cora's gonna kill me!" Lucky cried.

Bob ran up the pulley rope. Lucky lunged for him, grabbed onto the rope, and swung out like a trapeze performer. She grazed the portrait, accidentally tearing it on contact.

"Whoops. Sorry, Grandpa!" Lucky said to the portrait.

She fixed her eyes back on Bob. She was ever so close. His beady eyes widened. Lucky grabbed at the squirrel, but her hand closed one second too late. Bob jumped, gliding down, down, down toward the party below.

"Oh great, you can fly now?" Lucky said.

She swung down after Bob toward the center of the room. She swept across the tables, hanging upside down and knocking over candles and champagne bottles. Bottle corks popped like fireworks, rocketing across the room. But Lucky didn't let go. She was finally close to Bob again. He was just a few inches away. Still upside down, she grabbed an ice bucket from the table, ready to catch him.

"Now I've got you!" she said.

"Senator Popham, wait until you try the cake," Grandpa's voice said. Lucky heard Aunt Cora gasp.

Lucky turned to see Grandpa, Aunt Cora, and a group of his esteemed guests standing in the doorway. She was in for it now.

"Hi, Grandpa!" Lucky waved, sheepishly. The floor-length curtains behind her erupted into flames from a candle she had knocked over. The kitchen staff rushed into the room with pots full of water to put out the fire.

"Mistakes were made?" Lucky said, turning red.

Grandpa looked about the same color, ready to explode. Before he could say a word, his portrait came crashing down in front of him. Bob the squirrel came flying from across the room. *Splat!* He landed right on Grandpa's face.

"*Ahhh!*" Grandpa yelled.

With a click and a flash, a photographer captured the moment in an instant. Lucky hoped this would soon be no more than another memory to add to her collection of family photographs.

CHAPTER 2

Lucky sat across from Aunt Cora. She
listened to the *chug chug* of the Prescott Express Train and
glanced out the window at the sun-drenched sky. A first-
class cabin afforded them privacy, but Aunt Cora didn't look
up for talking. Instead, she stared at a newspaper in horror.
The headline on the front page read SHOULD PRESCOTT GIVE
UP? They'd published the photo of the squirrel plastered on
Grandpa's face across the spread.

"Front page is good, right?" Lucky said.

"Usually." Aunt Cora looked as if she might faint.

"I mean, if anyone can pull off a squirrel on his face, it's
Grandpa. He'll speak to us again eventually, right? Once—
you know—his face heals?"

"Grandpa just needs some peace and quiet to get his campaign back on track. We can go home at the end of summer," she said.

"Why so long?" Lucky had gone from prisoner to exile.

"Why? Because the mansion is still somewhat underwater, along with most of my fondest childhood memories," Aunt Cora admonished. A few pots of water had not been enough to control Lucky's "mistake."

"I said I was sorry," Lucky said for the millionth time. Her million-and-first apology was interrupted by the cabin door opening. A lady with a little growling dog stood there.

"Mr. Twinkles, what are these people doing in our cabin?" the woman, whom Lucky assumed to be Mr. Twinkles's owner, said. The little dog yapped in response.

Aunt Cora corrected her. "Oh, I'm terribly sorry but you must be mistaken. This is—" The little dog yapped again before Aunt Cora could finish. The woman shut the door with an angry slam.

Lucky laughed. "Mr. Twinkles! Did you see his little tie? He looks like he's all ready for the theater or something. Wait, do they have a theater where we're going?" She opened the window, trying to catch her breath. She looked out at a vast but very empty landscape. There was nothing but dirt and even bigger piles of dirt as far as she could see. "Or a library? Or a zoo? Or anything?"

The newspaper Aunt Cora was holding blew into her face. She stretched toward the window. "Let's keep the outside"—she managed to close the window—"outside, shall we?"

Lucky sighed. She pulled her feet up onto the seat and hugged her knees. She tried to get a little more comfortable in the stiff cabin.

"Feet!" Aunt Cora corrected her instantaneously. "We may be spending the summer in the wilderness, but we are not wild animals."

Lucky sighed again. She put her feet back onto the floor and slumped back into her chair. A small ball of apprehension and nervous energy formed in the pit of her stomach.

"What's it even like in...Mir*adro*?" She stumbled over the Spanish word that was the name of the city she'd been born in. Spanish was Lucky's first language, and while Aunt Cora had always made sure Lucky had an opportunity to practice it with her tutors at the Prescott mansion, those tutors didn't have the best accents. Lucky wished she could remember her mother's voice instead—cooing to her and singing her Mexican lullabies.

"Mir*adero*," Aunt Cora corrected.

"What am I supposed to call him?" Lucky said, voicing the worry that had been on her mind for days.

"Well, you can call him Dad! Or Father. Or Jim."

Lucky tried it on for size. "Jim. Hello, Jim. How have the last ten years been, Jim?" It felt awkward rolling from her tongue. It just didn't quite fit. The ball in her stomach was getting bigger.

She could see the sympathy in Aunt Cora's softening gaze. "Oh, honey. It wasn't easy for him after your mom died. Something *broke* in your father. And he..."

"Why didn't he come with me?"

"Sweetheart, he was alone in the wilderness with a baby. He did what he thought—well, what we *all* thought—was best."

The door opened again. A mustachioed passenger looked in. "Oh! This isn't the bathroom!" he said in a drawl.

"I beg your pardon!" Aunt Cora clutched her hand to her chest.

The man quickly shut the door, and Lucky tried to stifle more giggles.

"Really, Lucky." Aunt Cora sniffed.

The door opened again. Aunt Cora had had enough.

"This is a *private* cabin!" she said in a voice louder than usual.

This time it was the train conductor. Lucky recognized him from when they'd boarded the train. He closed the door quickly in surprise. Then, after a moment, he tentatively reopened the door and stuck his head back in. "Sorry.

Dining car closes in five minutes," he explained before closing the door again.

"Well. I believe it is time for some tea. Don't move," Aunt Cora said, composing herself. She stood and made her way out the door.

"The next stop is Miradero!" Lucky heard the conductor call from somewhere down the hall.

With no Aunt Cora there to chastise her, Lucky opened the window. Despite the barrenness of it all, there was something alluring about the landscape. Lucky stuck her head out and took a deep breath. The wind pulled the blue bow right out of her hair.

"Oh no!" Lucky lunged after it, but it was beyond the reach of her hands. Her eyes followed the ribbon as it got lost in the breeze. That's when she saw *him* and forgot all about her ribbon.

"It's a *wild horse!*" Lucky exclaimed.

A buckskin-colored mustang with a black mane galloped close to the train, running parallel to the tracks. Every so often he was partially obscured by the rocky hills that came into view. Lucky was mesmerized. She had never seen anything with such strength and power. The majestic creature raced unfettered across the open plain. He wasn't racing them. He was racing himself with the abandon of something truly free. Lucky gasped at the realization.

The train curved, bringing Lucky closer to the mustang. She was suddenly taken aback by the rumble of what must've been dozens of hooves. An entire herd of wild horses appeared in the distance. They were following the mustang.

"Whoa!" Lucky said.

The alpha horse caught up with the train. He was now outside Lucky's window. He looked at her. The proximity of the horse awakened something inside Lucky, and she laughed in amazement.

"This is so cool," she said to herself. The train turned another corner and she began to lose sight of the mustang.

"Oh no!" she said.

Lucky burst from her cabin and dashed down the train corridor. She pushed past the other passengers as she ran through the public train car, tracking the horse's every move through the large windows. She tripped on the snakeskin boot of a sleeping cowboy.

"Ow, hey—" the cowboy said, opening his eyes.

"Oh, sorry!" Lucky said.

She smacked another sleeping cowboy as she ran by, waking him, too.

"Hey, what'd you do that for, Handlebar? You know I have trouble sleeping," the second cowboy said, hitting the guy next to him.

"Hey. Huh? Wha—are we there? Get your elbow out of

my face, Walrus," Handlebar, a very strong-looking man, said. Walrus, the second cowboy, scuffled with Handlebar.

"Hey. What did I tell you about my private space, Walrus and Handlebar? Boss, he's bothering me again!" said another, very thin, cowboy.

"Shut up, Horseshoe. Fix your mustache," the first cowboy said. Lucky guessed that he was the boss from his tone of authority.

"Excuse me," Lucky said.

She didn't have time for this. She shifted her gaze to the horse and took off again. Lucky threw open the doors leading to the connector platform. She was out of breath, but she kept going. She moved to enter the next car but saw Aunt Cora sitting inside. Lucky ducked and tried to determine her next move.

She didn't want to say goodbye to the horse just yet. If she couldn't continue through the train, she would just have to go around the outside of it. Lucky climbed onto the side of the train, the wind whipping around at twenty-five miles per hour. At least that's what her math problem had said; it felt much faster than that. Lucky couldn't help thinking that this was probably what being in a tornado felt like. She held on to the train tight and locked eyes with the horse. He was close enough to touch now.

Lucky heard Aunt Cora's voice and remembered that her

aunt was just inside the train car. She looked through the window and saw Aunt Cora standing by the pastry tables.

"Cake, *mmhmm*, let's see. Chocolate. Lemon. *Ooh!* Coconut—" Cora reached for a pastry, but Mr. Twinkles's owner beat her to it.

"Oh, you are such a good boy! Yes, you are. Yes, you are!" the woman said, putting the plate on the floor for Mr. Twinkles.

Aunt Cora looked momentarily indignant before selecting another pastry. She took a bite just as she noticed Lucky out the window. Aunt Cora spit out her mouthful of cake and screamed, the cake hitting Mr. Twinkles's owner right in her face. Aunt Cora opened the window and leaned out for a better look.

"Lucky! Oh! Lucky!" she cried.

Lucky sidestepped the length of the train car, jumping onto the platform and through the door of the next car to close the gap between her and the magnificent horse. She bolted down the corridor, knocking over more passengers in her haste to reach the back of the train before it was too late.

"Oh! Whoops! Woo-o, whoops! Oh, oh, oh!" Aunt Cora said as she ran to catch up with Lucky. The little dog chased after her, yapping angrily. He nipped at her heels. "You wicked little dog."

"Mr. Twinkles! Down, boy!" his owner called.

Lucky finally made it to the caboose and moved through it to the very back end of the train while holding tightly to the railings. She looked up and saw the herd of horses led by the mustang running closely behind the train.

"Whoa!" she said.

She leaned over the railing and reached for the horse. She stretched her fingertips as far as they would go. She was eye to eye with the horse now. Their eyes connected. Was this what freedom felt like?

The train hit a bump in the tracks. Lucky slipped. She closed her eyes, bracing herself for the fall, but a hand pulled her back to safety. She looked up. It was the first cowboy she'd tripped over.

"Hey, hey, whoa! Watch yourself there, princess. You'll make someone real unhappy if you go diving overboard like that. You best just stay away from them wild horses, all right?" he said with a wink.

Aunt Cora appeared at that very moment, as if summoned.

"Lucky! There you are!" she said.

"Aunt Cora, I'm—"

She grabbed Lucky by the shoulders.

"You're going to be the end of me," Cora said. Then she looked up at the cowboy. "I'm much obliged, Mister...?"

The man tipped his hat. "The name is Hendricks, ma'am."

Aunt Cora ushered Lucky back inside. "I should put you on a leash, you know? And I'm going to. I'm going to put you on a leash," she said.

"*Ooh*, just a second! Wait!"

Lucky stopped in her tracks. She looked out the caboose window and stared longingly at the horse. He drifted farther and farther away until he was a speck of dust in the distance.

CHAPTER 3

The train whistled, announcing their arrival at their destination. Aunt Cora stood and opened the cabin door. Luggage and livestock filled the corridor and crisscrossed in all directions, nearly running her over. Lucky stayed in her seat, deciding it was best to stay out of the way until the coast was clear. She watched the bustle of the train station from the cabin window.

A man burst from the train and ran off into the station. "*Ooh, ooh!* You can find the toilets, Chevron," he said to himself, squirming. He opened the bathroom door, and a woman's scream rang out into the station. "Ah. Sorry, ma'am!" he said. He crossed over to the occupied men's bathroom and waited outside the door, still squirming.

Other train passengers walked off the train and followed the crowd into station.

"Just remember: Be yourself. Be your best self. Be the you that doesn't start fires," Aunt Cora said to Lucky from the corridor. She looked over her shoulder at Lucky, but Lucky wasn't there. "Lucky? I'm too young for gray hair."

A few more men crossed the aisle. Aunt Cora walked back into the cabin to find Lucky still sitting there. Her face softened empathetically. "Hey. Don't worry. He's really looking forward to seeing you. And I bet you the summer will go by much faster than you think," she said.

Lucky sighed. Aunt Cora pulled a new ribbon from her handbag and put it in Lucky's hair. She smiled.

They stepped off the train together. They stood next to their suitcases and looked at their new surroundings. It was nothing like back home. It was "rustic," as Aunt Cora once called it. The two of them stuck out like sore thumbs. Aunt Cora looked very uncomfortable.

"*Ooh*. What's that smell?" she said, putting a gloved hand to her face.

A slimy wad of something landed near Aunt Cora's fine shoe. A llama crossed their path, led by a cowboy.

"Sorry, ma'am. He spits," the cowboy said. The cowboy spit, too, and walked on.

"Ughhhh." Aunt Cora looked mortified. Lucky was amused. She'd never seen a llama in person before.

"Don't worry, Aunt Cora, I bet the summer will go by faster than you think," Lucky said.

"Very funny."

Lucky looked around for her dad or father or Jim. The train depot was full of men. She spotted a man with the same blue eyes as Aunt Cora's. "Is that him?"

"No . . . I don't see him anywhere."

"Are we in the right place?"

Aunt Cora looked around. "Yes. Unfortunately. I'll go check if he's in his office. Don't move until I get back." She emphasized this with a look before she headed for the depot office.

Lucky sat on her luggage and waited. The sleeping cowboys from the train were among the last to exit. They stretched and scratched themselves as they walked by.

"I'm hungry," said the big one, Walrus.

"Yeah, where is the saloon?" said the thin one, Horseshoe.

"Yeah! I want some bacon," said the strong-looking one, Handlebar.

"Oh, I could go for a steak," said Walrus.

The man who had saved Lucky from herself in the unfortunate caboose incident stepped off the train after them.

She remembered he'd called himself Hendricks. Hendricks glanced at Lucky and tipped his hat to her as he walked by.

"Stay outta trouble now, princess," he drawled.

Hendricks reunited with the rest of the cowboys.

"Hey, this ain't the coast!" Horseshoe said to him.

"Change of plans, boys. We ran out of money," said Hendricks.

Horseshoe and Walrus looked around the small station. They grumbled under their mustaches.

"Hey, you know where they got money?" said Horseshoe. "Banks."

Hendricks looked around at all the people still lingering in the station. He motioned for the men to lower their voices.

"You remember how well that worked last time? Now, listen up—" Hendricks was interrupted by Mr. Twinkles barking up a storm. The little dog pulled his owner across the station. Hendricks spoke again once they had passed. "I saw some horses from the train that'll buy us our next ticket out of here. Now, get going—you'll earn that bacon."

"*Ooh*, I like bacon!" said Walrus.

"This is why you're in change, boss!" said Horseshoe. "Here comes Chevron."

The man who'd made a run for the bathroom joined the group. "Whew, woo. What'd I miss?" he asked.

The train whistle blew again. The train slowly pulled away from the station, revealing a small arena on the other side. The large sign at its entrance read MIRADERO RODEO. There were horses and crowds of people waving flags. Lucky walked toward it, completely forgetting Aunt Cora's explicit instructions not to move. Lucky's eyes weren't big enough to take it all in. It wasn't at all like back home. For one, there were people here who looked like Lucky and Milagro. The people around her were all shades of colors. Many of them sprinkled Spanish into their English. Or maybe it was English into their Spanish.

There were animals strolling around, too. A tiny burro trotted past her. A little fair-haired, freckled boy chased after it.

"It's your pal Snips! I promise I won't make you wear the dress again. Wait for me. Come back! I'm sorry," he said.

Lucky laughed. She felt utterly enchanted by it all. She hardly noticed the odd glances she was getting from passers-by over her dress.

"*Laaaaaadies* and gentlemen, mares and stallions," someone announced. Lucky followed the sound of the voice. "Let's give a warm round of applause to Valentina and Las Caballeras de Miradero! Brought to you by Granger's Corral: Stables so fine, you'll want to sleep there yourself!" a tall, dark-skinned man said. The man's booming voice switched tone. "Today's events are brought to you by Al Granger's Corral!" He gestured to himself to indicate that he was Al Granger and continued. "Breaking horses without breaking the bank. Come on down! Stable prices for stabled horses."

Lucky turned and turned, taking in a world so different from the one back home. At last, she stopped and focused on the ring in the center of the arena. A group of women with varying shades of brown skin and dark hair made their way to the center of the ring atop stallions. They wore beautiful ruffled shirts hemmed with colorful ribbons, accented by purple woven silk sashes. The ribbons and sashes waved slightly in the breeze. Lucky was mesmerized. Traditional Mexican music started in the background. The horsewomen and their stallions began to trot to the music. They picked up speed and wove intricate patterns through one another. Far too soon, the show ended and the crowd burst into cheers. The women and their stallions trotted out from the ring.

One of the horses came to an abrupt stop in front of Lucky.

"Whoa!" Lucky said. The rider fixed her eyes on Lucky as if she were seeing a ghost.

"Fortuna?" the horsewoman said.

"Uh...oh, um. ¡Hola! Buenos días." Lucky was polite

but confused. How did this woman know her name? Her *full* name at that. Was she supposed to know this woman?

"Of course you wouldn't remember me. I am Valentina. You look just like your mother," the rider explained to Lucky. She turned to the horsewoman behind her. "Doesn't she, Alta Gracia?"

"Si, te pareces a tu madre, pero mas blanquita," Alta Gracia said.

Lucky had never had anyone tell her that she looked like a lighter-skinned version of her mother before.

"Bienvenida, Fortuna!" Valentina said, and lightly tapped her stallion on his haunches with her spurs. The horse moved to leave.

"Wait, you knew her?" Lucky said, chasing after them.

"Everyone knew Milagro," interjected Alta Gracia. Valentina paused and looked down at Lucky with the kind of smile Lucky imagined only a mother had.

"Here—your mother would want you to have one of these. She had one just like it," Valentina said.

She untied the sash around her waist and tossed it to Lucky. Lucky stared at the colorful woven Mexican textile in her hand. Her mother was wearing a similar sash in the pictures Lucky had.

Alta Gracia nodded at Lucky in farewell and galloped past them.

"Welcome home, mi'ja," Valentina said, following Alta Gracia's lead.

Lucky watched them go, trying to make sense of the encounter. Had her mother been a Caballera de Miradero? And if her mother once had a sash like the one in her hands, where was it now?

The announcer, Al Granger, was at it again. "Next up, our very own Western Reigning Champ—and the champion of her old dad's heart—my daughter, Pru Granger, and the incomparable Chica *Lindaaa*!" he said. The crowd began to form again. A well-postured girl with long braided hair and skin the same rich shade as the announcer rode past the crowd on a breathtaking palomino. The rider looked to be about Lucky's age.

Lucky wove through the crowd in the direction of the ring, tracking the girl atop her horse. "Excuse me, coming through!" Lucky said. She pushed her way back to the side of the ring, where she spotted a barrel. She climbed onto it to get a better view.

Pru rode into the ring and the crowd burst into a cheer. Pru and Chica Linda speed-walked backward with remarkable precision, stopping on a dime. The audience applauded with gusto.

"Wow, that girl can ride!" a man said from somewhere behind Lucky.

Chica Linda balanced on one hoof. The pair spun like a toy top, dizzying the audience into another round of applause.

"She's been making my head spin for thirteen years, so I'm used to it!" Al Granger bellowed. "She doesn't do a thing unless she can do it perfectly."

Lucky watched in awe. "Whoa. Horses can do that?" she asked no one in particular.

"All right, you show-off! Ain't you got chores to get to?" Al Granger teased the girl. "Let's give it up for Miradero's blue-ribbon rider, Miss Pru Granger, aboard Chica *Lindaaaa*!" Pru and Chica Linda pranced to the center of the ring and took a bow. They soaked in the applause.

Lucky couldn't believe what she'd just seen. She stood there on the barrel with her mouth agape.

"Fortuna Esperanza Navarro Prescott! You get back here," a flustered Aunt Cora called from the other side of the livestock holding pens. She headed toward Lucky.

"Aunt Cora, you have to see this!" Lucky said.

Aunt Cora looked around for the fastest way to reach Lucky, not wanting to risk losing her again. She needed to cut across the holding pens, but there was no visible way in. So, with no other options, she lifted one of her legs over the fence.

Moo!

A cow startled Cora, and she lost her balance and fell into the pen. Picking herself up, Aunt Cora tried to tiptoe behind the cows to make her way out, but her movement tickled them and set off a chain reaction of tails swishing and swatting Aunt Cora. Lucky couldn't help giggling.

She wasn't the only one to notice Aunt Cora's misfortune.

"And here's our next contender! Feast your eyes on this filly. Now, those are some smooth moves." Al Granger signaled to Aunt Cora. He gave the crowd a play-by-play of her struggle to navigate through the livestock until she finally made it through. "And what a finale! Oh, don't try that at home, folks."

Aunt Cora straddled the fence again as she tried to exit the pen. "Ugh! Oh. Oh…," she said, trying to stay balanced this time.

A handsome cowboy appeared from nowhere and held out his hand. "May I offer you a hand there, ma'am?" he said.

Once again lacking any other options, Cora accepted. She took the cowboy's hand and he helped her over, tipping his hat once she was stable. Aunt Cora looked down, composing herself. She seemed to notice the dire condition of her dress for the first time. There was mud all over it. Aunt Cora dabbed at stains, but that only made the mess worse.

The cowboy whispered something Lucky couldn't hear close to Cora's ear. Aunt Cora blushed. "Well, I never," she said. She put her hands on her waist and sidestepped him.

"I'm sorry to hear that," the cowboy said with a flirtatious smile.

Aunt Cora was finally able to approach Lucky. Cora grabbed her by the hand and pulled her off the barrel. Together, they trudged back toward Main Street.

"Unbelievable. Stranding us at the station like common vagabonds," Aunt Cora said.

Lucky couldn't seem to pry her eyes away from the arena and the ring. "Did you see those amazing women riding those horses? One gave me this sash—"

"I need a strong cup of tea. And to burn this dress." Aunt Cora was deep in her own conversation.

Lucky tugged at her arm. "Aunt Cora, did you ever see my mom perform?"

"Yes. She was fearless," Aunt Cora answered. A cart topped with luggage went by. "Wait, sir! A ride?!" The man did not stop.

"Need a ride?" a small voice said, all salesman.

It was the fair-haired boy with the burro Lucky had seen earlier. He switched the sign hanging from his donkey from TELEGRAMS to FORTUNES TOLD to RIDES.

"Snips is the name," he continued. "Rides, tours, and

telegrams are my game! And this noble steed is Señor Carrots, my business partner. Where to, ma'ams?"

Aunt Cora looked exhausted. She glanced down at the tiny burro with apprehension. "Thank you, no. But if you could just point us in the direction of the Prescott house?" she said.

"I'll getcha there in a jiffy for just a penny," Snips said. He pushed Aunt Cora onto the mini-burro's back. Señor Carrots looked ready to topple over. It did not look safe.

"No, uh-uh, no, *uhh*!" Aunt Cora protested.

"All aboard! Toot, toot! Next stop, Prescott House," Snips said. Señor Carrots took a few steps and then stopped. Snips urged him onward, but the burro refused to go any farther. "C'mon," the boy muttered. Señor Carrots looked away.

Accepting defeat, Snips said, "Okay. Here we are. In a jiffy, as advertised. Your destination, just ahead."

The boy pointed. Cora and Lucky followed his gesture to a farmhouse that sat perched on top of the hill.

"That'll be one penny," the boy continued. He held out his free hand for payment.

"Okay." Aunt Cora said. She looked happy to just be on her own two feet again. She placed a penny in Snips's hand.

"Snips! You little thief!" yelled a girl who looked about Lucky's age.

Her hair was so blond, it was almost white. But that was not the most noticeable thing about her: She wore pants and rode a red-brown and white pinto horse!

Snips yelped. "Uh-oh. You saw nothing. Enjoy your stay," he said. He jumped on Señor Carrots. "Like the wind," he commanded.

The girl stood up in her stirrups and swung a lasso overhead. "You better stop harassing those nice people," she said.

Snips tried to escape but was yanked right off his burro by the perfectly aimed lasso. Señor Carrots looked around, baffled, and took off running. The girl jumped off her horse and began hog-tying the boy.

"*Ahh!* Oh no, no. Hey, stop! Ah!" Snips said.

The girl looked up at Lucky for the first time. "Ohmigosh, you must be Lucky Prescott! I like your hair. And your dress." She talked a mile a minute. "Oh and your shoes. I didn't know shoes could be cute. Can I try them on? Sorry about my brother."

"I'm the one you ought to apologize to. Hey, stop," Snips interrupted. The girl covered his mouth and smiled awkwardly.

"Oh, um, here." She reached down and took the penny out of Snips's shirt pocket and handed it to Aunt Cora. Aunt Cora didn't say a thing. She proceeded to examine

31

the extent of the damage to her dress. The girl turned back to Lucky. "I'm Abigail. This is my best friend, Boomerang. Say hello, Boomerang. . . ." The horse seemed to smile. Abigail spoke in a horselike voice. "It's a pleasure to meet you, madame."

"It's nice to meet you, too," Lucky said to Boomerang. She laughed.

Al Granger's voice carried out to them as he announced the next act. "No one can beat the barrel-racing clock better than Miss Abigail Stone. . . ."

"Uh-oh, I'm up," Abigail said. She jumped back on her horse.

"Bye!" Lucky waved. "Good luck out there."

The boy still lay on the ground, tied into a ball. "Abigail! You can't leave me here!" he said.

A gun popped, signaling the start of the race. Boomerang took off, rodeo-style.

"Watch me! See ya later," Abigail said.

Aunt Cora finally looked up. Her face was streaked with dirt. She looked miserable. "I think the donkey ate part of my dress," she said.

CHAPTER 4

Aunt Cora and Lucky walked up a dirt path to the house on the hill. Lucky couldn't stop talking about the rodeo show. "She was my age and she was on this beautiful horse, and did you know horses could walk backward? It's like—" Lucky stopped mid-sentence as they came upon the Prescott house.

It was an idyllic farmhouse with lovely trees and a porch that seemed out of place in the dusty town of Miradero. Lucky was suddenly transported to another time. She'd studied the house in pictures...but maybe she also remembered it.

"Ah, at last. Civilization!" Aunt Cora said.

A breeze ruffled Lucky's hair. She looked in the direction

of the breeze and saw a swing hanging from a tree, rocking back and forth with a creak. It was the same swing from the photo of her and her parents. Lucky walked to it and sat down on the bench. She smiled and let the breeze sway her, overwhelmed with finally seeing the house again in person.

Aunt Cora was already at the door. She knocked. No answer. "Jim?" she called. She walked down the porch and peeked in the windows. "Jim Prescott," she said more forcefully. Still no answer. Cora found a barrel on the side of the house and climbed up on it. She called to the upstairs window. "James Prescott Jr.! *Jiiiim!*" She was yelling now. Nothing.

Cora pulled an apple from a nearby barrel. Lucky noticed that the trees around the house were apple trees. She was surprised that there was enough of a frost in Miradero for apples to grow. Aunt Cora tossed the apple up to the second-floor window, but it got stuck in the tree branches above her.

Lucky continued to swing. She spotted a man coming from an adjacent barn. He wiped something off his hands with a rag. Lucky's smile faded. This older, grease-stained, grim-faced man did not look like the smiling dad from her photographs. The man laid his eyes on Aunt Cora, who was bending to grab another apple.

"Cora," Jim said.

Aunt Cora froze mid-bend. She pulled herself back together and saw her brother for the first time in a long time. "Oh! Jim," she said.

Jim's eyes widened and panned the front yard. They landed on his daughter, sitting on the yard swing. "Lucky," he said.

He froze. He didn't seem to know what to do. Neither did Lucky. She waved awkwardly. Jim looked back at Aunt Cora. No one spoke. The silence seemed to go on forever. The apple Aunt Cora threw earlier dislodged from the tree and fell squarely on Jim's head. This snapped him out of his reverie. He laughed and turned on a welcoming charm.

"I can't believe you guys are here! How was the trip?" He gritted his teeth and muttered the next part directly to Aunt Cora. "I thought you were coming on the twentieth."

Aunt Cora rolled her eyes before smiling sweetly. "It *is* the twentieth, little brother," she said.

"Oh. Right. Well, that explains it," he said.

Jim made his way up the porch of the house. Aunt Cora and Lucky followed him. Jim started to open the front door, but something crashed inside. A train part rolled out. Jim turned to face them once more.

"The house—it's not—I'm not ready," he said. "Uh…"

"Oh for goodness' sake," Aunt Cora said.

She pushed Jim inside the house. Lucky and Cora paused in the doorway, taking in the bachelor pad. What it lacked in warmth, it made up for in train parts. Nevertheless, Jim had clearly made some kind of an effort. It was cluttered but clean. There was even a pillow or two on the benches. Lucky stepped inside. She had a sudden sense of memory, as if she knew this place. Though she realized it probably hadn't looked anything like this when she had lived there.

Jim moved a few errant train parts out of the way before turning around.

"Yeah. Home sweet home. Uh, mi casa es su casa," he said in an accent that wasn't nearly as good as it should be for someone living in Miradero. "Just step on over that one. Yeah, you can just...Sorry about that. I bring my work home with me," he said. "There is more, of course. Ah. We eat there," he gestured toward the kitchen. "And, *umm*, the sleeping is upstairs. Uh, I can show you your room."

He turned to Lucky apologetically. It seemed like nothing was coming out the way he wanted. He zipped his mouth and picked up their suitcases. Lucky followed him up the stairs.

"Watch your step," he continued as they navigated the maze of train parts. "Don't want those falling on any toes.

Solid iron. Safer than the old strap-rail tracks, but much heavier."

Lucky could see that talking trains was his comfort zone. He was a true engineer. Lucky wanted to hear more, but Jim already seemed lost in his own head.

Meanwhile, Aunt Cora looked just about done in. She backed up into a stack of crates next to the stairs and sat down.

"Don't get near those boxes, Cora. Highly explosive," Jim called.

Aunt Cora jumped up, looking at the side of the crates: DYNAMITE. She shook her head at Jim, but he was already upstairs. Lucky followed him to the top floor of the house, the attic.

"So, uh. This is your room. What do you think?" he asked. He opened the window to let in some air.

Lucky took it all in. It was musty and very... fruity. The walls were plastered with strawberry wallpaper, the bed held strawberry pillows, and the corner even sported a chair decorated with strawberries.

"Uh, that's a lot of strawberries," she said.

Jim set down her suitcase. He looked confused. He quickly snatched up a strawberry toy from the edge of the bed and hid it behind his back. "Oh, *umm, hmm*. You like strawberries. Right?"

"I do?" said Lucky.

"Oh, okay. Well, you used to." There was an awkward silence again.

"Oh. Huh," Lucky said, giving the room another once-over.

"Yep. You were like...you were like this." He held up the toy to suggest how small she was. "But now you're, now you're like this." He raised his hand to illustrate how tall she was. "So...*umm.*" He threw the toy aside. Lucky could see that he had tried his best to connect with the version of her that he remembered.

"Well, uh, I'll let you unpack and get settled." His eyes fixed on the sash in her hands and opened wide. His face suddenly sagged with a mix of sadness and fear. "Where'd you get that?" He pointed at the fabric.

"Uh, a woman at the rodeo gave it to me."

"Oh. Las Caballeras. They used to ride with your mother."

"Right. Yeah, they actually said I look just like her—"

"Well," he interrupted. Something dark passed over his face. It was too much, too soon. "There are, uh, extra sheets in the hall. Uh, towels."

Jim made his way from the room. He paused at the top of the stairs, his back to Lucky. Lucky wondered if having her there looking so much like her mother was making the memories flood back for him, just as this house was for her. He looked as if he were drowning. He turned to Lucky, taking a deep breath.

"Yeah, you do, uh...look just like her," he said before he disappeared.

Lucky stared at the empty stairs, confused. Shouldn't the memories of his mother make him happy? She opened her suitcase and sighed. It was filled with city shoes and dresses she pulled out to hang. When she opened the wardrobe, she saw a tiny beam of light shining through the back panel. Lucky squinted, peering through a hollow knot in the wood. She gasped.

There was a room on the other side.

From what Lucky could see, the room was very colorful. The walls were lined with clothing, costumes, cowgirl hats, a poster. She pulled away and pushed the wardrobe with all her strength until it slid out of the way. She yelped in victory.

Lucky stood at the threshold of what seemed like another reality. She stepped inside the vibrant room, amazed. But as she moved to further explore, something tugged the hem of her dress. Lucky looked and saw she was caught on a trunk engraved with her mother's name: Milagro. Lucky pulled her skirt free and stepped to the poster she'd seen through the knot. It showed Milagro standing on a horse. Lucky was mesmerized by it. The Milagro on the poster wore a sash like the one Lucky still held in her hands. She realized she must be standing in her mother's dressing room.

A gust of wind blew through the open window and into the room. Lucky heard the sound of something turning: *tic-tic-tic*. She looked around and saw that the sound was coming from something spinning inside a wooden contraption on Milagro's dresser. There was a tiny eyehole on the thing. Lucky leaned in to look through it. The breeze continued to spin it. Lucky saw Milagro riding her horse before her very eyes.

"Mama!" She gasped.

Seeing her mother this way felt like magic. In reality, Lucky was looking into a zoetrope—a device that displayed a sequence of photographs to create the illusion of motion. A horse whinnied outside, making the moving images seem that much more alive. The sound of the horse became louder. Curious, Lucky leaned out the window to listen intently. She heard the whinny in the distance again. It sounded familiar. Lucky wondered if there was a chance that this was the same horse from the train.

Deciding to find out for herself, Lucky made her way downstairs. She passed Aunt Cora in the kitchen, where she was rummaging through the cupboards. Cora paused to stare at a box of dynamite beside a box of produce on the floor and shook her head in disapproval.

"Oh, Jim, Jim, Jim," she said.

"I'm gonna go explore," Lucky called to her as she rushed outside.

"Yeah, it's probably safer outdoors," Aunt Cora said, sidestepping the box of dynamite.

CHAPTER 5

Lucky made her way into town. She followed the sign that pointed to Main Street as well as the sound of the horse. Soon, she came upon a corral with a barn sitting adjacent to it. Lucky heard that familiar whinny coming from the other side of the barn doors. She also heard kicking and grunting and what sounded like an army of men.

The girl who had performed at the rodeo walked up to the corral. She poured water into a trough, eyeing Lucky. "You're Lucky Prescott, right?" the girl asked.

"Hi," Lucky said.

"Pru Granger."

"I know. I saw you at the rodeo. You were amazing." There was no way Lucky could forget.

"Thanks, but I totally messed up my rein back. I'll get it right for the festival at the end of summer."

Lucky could hardly hear Pru over the growing commotion in the barn. The barn doors kicked open. Lucky didn't see any horses, but she recognized the men from the train.

"Look out, boys! That's the wildest horse I've ever seen," Walrus said.

"Take it easy there, fella," Horseshoe cajoled.

"Watch out for the tail!" Walrus said.

"Ah, ahh, ahh!" Chevron said, resorting to the same dance from his search for a toilet. He looked ready to pee himself this time, too.

"We got a biter!" Horseshoe said.

"Well, bite him back. Let's go!" Hendricks ordered.

"I think he's too much horse for you, Horseshoe," Handlebar said.

"You try keeping him still," Horseshoe whined.

"Step aside." Hendricks pushed his men out of the way. "Eyes on the prize there, boys! This one will sell for a good price."

"Come on. We can't hold him forever," Handlebar said.

"Ow! Son of a daisy," Chevron cried.

"When he's broke, he'll be worth a lot of money," Hendricks reminded them. "Hold him!"

"Hang on there, big guy," Horseshoe said.

"Hold him, *oof*—ow!" Handlebar grunted.

They argued among themselves. The walls of the barn were practically shaking. Lucky turned to Pru. "Is that barn going to be okay?" she said with a nervous laugh.

"Should hold tight. Those clowns rented the corral to break a wild horse they brought with them," Pru said.

"Break?" Lucky reached her hand to her face. They were going to break that beautiful horse. She felt mortified. The color drained from her.

"It's not as bad as it sounds," Pru said. A loud, high-pitched scream came from the barn. Pru winced. That did not reassure Lucky that breaking a horse was a humane process. Could a human even make a sound like that? Pru climbed onto the fence, straining her neck to see. "It's not that bad for the *horse*, anyway."

"Ow! He bit off my mustache," Chevron cried.

"Whoa! Look out! *Look out!*" Horseshoe warned.

"Son of a daisy—" Walrus grunted.

"Whoa! Look out! I can't hold him!" Handlebar echoed.

"Wait! The saddle's not tight!" Chevron whimpered.

The men spilled from the barn, scurrying like roaches. Chevron was in fact missing *half* his mustache. The horse burst through the barn doors behind them, a wild bronco bucking while Hendricks held on. Lucky's jaw dropped in horror. It was indeed the same horse from the train.

"Yeehaw! Hee-yaa! Woo! That all you got? Come on! Yeehaw! Let's see what you're made of," Hendricks bellowed. He was clearly the pro in the group. He dug his spurs deep into the horse's sides to amp him up. "Come on." Hendricks laughed.

"Stop! You're hurting him!" Lucky yelled. Hendricks didn't so much as bat an eye at her. He was too immersed in the battle of wills.

"Oh, yeah, that's not right," Pru whispered to Lucky. "Hold on." She ran to the side of the barn.

The horse bucked wildly in the middle of the corral. He seemed to enjoy the challenge. Hendricks somehow managed to hold on. He was enjoying it, too. He smiled and laughed.

"If that's how you want to play it, all right. Oh, you kicking big now," he said to the horse. He dug his spurs even deeper.

The horse huffed as if he'd had enough fun for one day. Then he reared back and threw Hendricks off, sending him flying into the fence in front of Lucky. "Wahh! *UMPH!*" Hendricks cried.

"Hendricks, look out!" Handlebar said. The horse charged forward at Hendricks, who scrambled over the fence to Lucky's side.

Hendricks put his arms out in front of him. "Whoa, whoa, whoa, *whoa!*" he said.

The horse stopped just short of the fence, launching the saddle off his back. Hendricks dodged, but it clipped him anyway. A vengeful look darkened his eyes.

"You crazy horse," he muttered.

"Looks like you're the one getting broken today, Hendricks," Horseshoe said.

"Yeah, we'll see about that," Hendricks retorted, spinning around. He then seemed to notice Lucky for the first time. "Why, hello there, princess." Lucky scoffed. "See, I told you: These horses right here, they're dangerous. You best just run along now," he said before turning his full attention back to the horse.

"Quick, get a rope on him!" Horseshoe said. "On your left! Oh, get in front of him. Get in front of him!"

"Cut him off! Cut him off!" Handlebar barked.

"Now, who's the knucklehead that didn't strap this saddle on right? Bunch of dimwits." Hendricks chided his men. He jumped over the fence, back into the corral.

"It wasn't me!" the men said over one another.

The horse chased Handlebar through the corral. "Whoa! *Waaa!* Get him away from me!" he cried, protecting his backside with his hands.

"Dang horse, do you ever give up?" Hendricks said. "Rope 'im," he commanded the men, and flung his lasso. The men followed. Three ropes landed around the horse's neck, one by one.

"Oh, I got him!" Horseshoe exclaimed. "I got him. I got him! Hold up there, big guy!"

"Whoa, whoa!" Chevron yelled. "Pick up the slack!"

"Change of plans, boys. Let's just get this animal under control, shall we?" Hendricks said. He pulled out a bull-whip and cracked it.

Pru turned the corner just in time. She gave Lucky a look that seemed to say, *They're in for it now.* Al Granger, her father and owner of the Granger Corral, trailed behind her.

"Hey! Whoa, whoa there, boys," Al Granger bellowed. "I don't know where you boys rode in from, but in my corral, we treat horses with respect. You don't like it, you can move along. Are we clear?" Hendricks dropped the whip. He signaled for his men to stop. They eased their pull on the ropes.

"Yessir, we are absolutely clear. Sure thing, boss," Hendricks said. He snuck a sly look to his men. Then he turned up the charm. "We didn't mean for it to get out of hand. This mustang's just got a lot of...spirit. All right, boys. Let's call it a day. Give this horse a rest."

Chevron climbed onto the outside of the fence. He used

48

the fence as leverage, pulling the horse toward him. "Hoo-wee!" he cried.

Horseshoe joined him. "Hold still. All right, give me a hand here," he called to the other men. They pulled on the ropes together with enough restraint that Al Granger looked satisfied. He walked back around the barn to whatever task he'd been at before Pru called on him.

"We'll come back tomorrow. When he's nice and thirsty," Hendricks said under his breath once the horse was contained and tied to a post.

He kicked over the water trough and gave the horse one last sinister look as he walked away. Lucky's eyes narrowed at Hendricks. She could see him for what he was now. She wasn't falling for his good-guy act from the train. The rest of the men walked away chuckling. Lucky thought that only a heartless person could laugh like that after what they'd done.

"Boys, we have our tickets outta here. I can taste the steak already. I like mine well-done," Hendricks said.

"I like steak!" Walrus interrupted.

"Boy, do I hurt. Does anyone have any Epsom salts?" Chevron moaned. The rest of their voices faded away as they moved out of sight.

Pru jumped back into the corral and stared at the empty trough she'd just filled. She groaned. "Ugh. Charming."

The horse looked miserable. Lucky slowly approached the post he was tied to. She was pained by what those men had done to him. The horse reared up, as if fighting an invisible enemy or the memories of the men who had tied him there. Whatever it was, it was undeniably powerful and intimidating, from the dark look in the horse's eyes. His hooves thundered back down to earth and his nostrils flared as he eyed Lucky. Their eyes connected again, and it dawned on Lucky that what she'd felt this entire time was recognition. She saw herself in this wild horse.

"You *do* have a lot of spirit," she cooed.

The horse breathed heavily. Lucky took a step closer, and he stared at her warily. She held up one arm to show him she meant no harm. Lucky's heart beat fast as she reached out to unhook the rope from the post with her other hand. The second the rope eased, the horse bolted to the opposite side of the corral. Lucky understood the feeling. She'd often felt that way back at the Prescott mansion.

Lucky looked at the spilled trough and Pru. The horse was going to need water. "You want help filling that back up?" she asked.

"Oh, no way. I wouldn't want you to get your dress dirty, city girl," Pru said. It wasn't a dig. She smiled at Lucky.

"What? This thing? *Pfft*." Lucky knotted up the bottom

of her dress so that her legs were free to move. She cut across the corral.

"Okay, then." Pru laughed. She handed Lucky a bucket. Lucky took it gladly. That horse needed water. She and Pru walked to the barn together.

CHAPTER 6

Lucky sat at the kitchen table later with Aunt Cora and Jim. Jim passed the mashed potatoes. Aunt Cora passed the steak. Lucky thought that Jim having to fend for himself in the kitchen all these years had really paid off. Aunt Cora never so much as set foot in the kitchen of the Prescott mansion in all her years of living there. Lucky imagined the situation was similar for Jim when he lived there. Nevertheless, the dinner he'd fixed was impressive.

"Wait, wait, wait, let me get this straight. The squirrel came down the stairs in the middle of his campaign speech and landed on Father's face? The Honorable James Prescott?" Jim said.

Lucky couldn't tell if he was disappointed in her, so she

sat there with her mouth full of mashed potatoes. She wasn't sure whether to deny or confirm.

"*Yeaaa*—maybe?" she said at last, and only so she could fill her mouth with more of those delicious potatoes.

There was a long pause. Then Jim burst into laughter.

"That's the funniest thing I've ever heard." He was practically in tears, laughing. Lucky started to chuckle, too.

"Yeah, one minute he was all"—she deepened her voice to impersonate her grandpa—"'The family motto is my campaign promise to you....'"

"Oh! Oh!" Jim held his sides.

"*Prescotts never give up,*" he and Lucky said in unison.

"And then the squirrel jumped on his face and he screamed!" Lucky gestured with such excitement that the mashed potatoes on the spoon she was holding went flying across the table, splattering onto Aunt Cora's face.

"*Ahh!*" Aunt Cora screamed.

"Sorry, Aunt Cora," Lucky said.

So much for their fun. She braced herself for a lecture... but then Aunt Cora burst into laughter, too. The potatoes dripped from her face onto her plate. This made them all laugh even more. Lucky got up and tried to dab at Aunt Cora's dress with her napkin.

"Oh, I think that was just overdue payback for some of the food fights your Aunt Cora started back in—" Jim began.

"I have no idea what you're talking about. I think we've told enough stories for one night, don't you, Jim?" Aunt Cora interrupted. She gave him an "older sister" look. Jim nodded.

"So, Lucky. How—how was your first day exploring Miradero?" he asked, changing the subject.

"Great. I made some friends," Lucky said. Aunt Cora squealed. Lucky didn't pay mind to her apparent surprise. "Well, I hope we'll be friends. One's kind of shy...and he's a little wild."

"Wild?" Aunt Cora asked with a hint of concern.

"What's his name? Where's he live?" Jim grunted. He looked about ready to fight someone.

Lucky took a second to think about what *his* name was. He didn't have a name so far as she knew. Or maybe he did, but it certainly wasn't a human one. Lucky had to think quickly, because Jim looked increasingly as if he was about to boil over.

"His name is...Spirit," Lucky said, officially naming him. "We met on the train. Well, outside the train, technically."

Aunt Cora listened pensively. Jim looked on, confused. "What kind of name is that, anyway?" he said.

"You mean that wild horse?" Aunt Cora asked. She had connected the dots.

Jim's eyes opened wide. He pushed his chair back from the table. He was way more worked up than when they'd thought she was talking about a boy. "The one in Al's corral?" Jim said. Lucky wanted to say, *Yes, that's the one*, but Jim's face was practically changing colors. It was now purple. "No."

"No, what?" Lucky said.

"You will not go near that horse again. Ever," Jim said.

Lucky was shocked. She looked to Aunt Cora, who had acted as good as a parent for the past ten years. But Aunt Cora hung her head as if someone had just died. It suddenly dawned on Lucky that someone actually *had*.

This was about her mother and the way she'd died all those years ago.

"But why?" Lucky asked in protest. "It's not Spirit's fault Mama fell off a horse!"

"No, no. You don't know what you're talking about. You stay away from that horse. No horses." Jim made it clear. He wasn't backing down. But Lucky didn't want to back down, either. Jim sighed. Aunt Cora looked at them both with compassion.

"I'm full," Lucky said. She stood from the table defiantly.

"Ah, okay." Jim stood up, too, and walked out, slamming the door.

Aunt Cora remained at the table alone while Lucky carried

her plate to the kitchen. She held in the tears until she could run up the stairs to the attic, where she could be alone. Once she was in her room, she glanced at the poster of her mother and cried for the first time in a long time.

Lucky walked down to breakfast the next morning. She found Aunt Cora in the kitchen, draping the tablecloth over the kitchen table. She set the table with eggs, pancakes, and all the fixings. She hummed to herself, as if it were a normal day.

"*Mmm*, pancakes," Lucky said.

"Breakfast?" Aunt Cora asked.

"My favorite." Lucky grabbed a plate. Jim entered with a platter full of pancakes. Of course, *he* had made breakfast. Lucky pushed her plate away. "I'm not hungry," she said. She stood up and made her way to the door.

"Lucky?" Aunt Cora said. Lucky paused and looked back at her. "If you're going out, you can pick up some groceries. Jim here isn't going to be the only one cooking." Aunt Cora gave her a bag and some money. She began jotting down a list.

"I guess I'm going to go check on my guys at the station—maybe they'll have breakfast with me," Jim said.

He walked out of the house quietly. Cora sighed. At last,

she handed Lucky the list. Lucky grabbed it and ran out the door without a goodbye.

Lucky hurried into town. She glanced at the buildings, trying to figure out where to go. Then she spotted a sign on a small building that read MERCADO. That was the Spanish word for "market." Lucky paused in front of the store for a moment. Then she pivoted and ran in the direction of Granger's Corral.

When she arrived, Pru and Al Granger were tossing bales of hay onto a wagon just outside the barn. Lucky stood a bit too close.

"Dad, be careful," Pru said.

"Oh! Sorry," Al said, noticing Lucky. He wiped his hand on his shirt and extended it to her for a vigorous shake. "Well, Lucky Prescott."

"Thanks for all your help yesterday," Pru said.

"Hey. Yeah, no problem," Lucky said.

"Where are you off to at such a gallop?" Al Granger said.

Lucky was there to see Spirit, of course, but she didn't know if she should say that. Pru's dad might tell hers.

Instead, she side-eyed Spirit and racked her brain for an excuse. "I was...I was just...*umm*...getting some groceries for Aunt Cora." That was the honest truth.

"Well, you're a bit turned around. Grocer's back that

way," Al Granger said, pointing back to where she'd come from.

"Oh. Yes. Okay, thanks," Lucky said. She would have to come back later. She turned bashfully and headed back to the mercado. She could hear Pru and her dad bantering warmly behind her.

"I get to drive!" Pru said.

"Okay, but don't tell your mother. She'll have my hide," Al Granger said.

Lucky couldn't help wishing her family were a little more like that. She didn't feel good about how she'd left things with Jim.

The mercado sat on Main Street. It was a one-room building that looked much like a barn inside. The proprietor was an older Mexican gentleman. Lucky handed him Aunt Cora's list.

"Aquí y aquí," he said in a soft-spoken manner as he showed Lucky where the items were and helped her fill her bag.

Lucky wondered if this is what Abuelo, her grandfather on her mother's side, would've been like. She'd never met anyone on her mother's side of the family. Lucky thanked the man. "Gracias," she said.

"De nada," the man replied.

Lucky headed outside with her heavy bag and saw Hendricks and his men walking up Main Street in her direction. They were deep in conversation and did not notice her. Lucky ducked behind a barrel outside of the mercado to listen.

"So what time does the midnight express come in?" Walrus asked.

"Midnight, dummy." Hendricks cuffed him on the head.

"Security's looser than my grandpappy's teeth," Horseshoe said. "Just the old man and his llama."

"I don't like llamas," Walrus said.

"All right, then," Hendricks said.

Lucky waited for them to disappear into the distance and then ran down Main Street. She tried to move fast, but the bag of groceries was heavy. She heard Spirit whinny as she got closer. He sounded distressed. The sound hurt her heart. She picked up speed.

She dropped her bag by the fence and approached the corral cautiously. She climbed onto the fence and untied Spirit from the post.

"Hey, hey, easy now. Easy. It's all right, boy. All this new stuff is kind of scary, huh?" She said that second part to herself. "I think we'll be okay. Trust me." Spirit reared up. Lucky stumbled back, surprised.

"Hey, city girl! Careful. This is a wild one," Pru said. Lucky hadn't noticed her come up next to her on the fence.

"Yeah, he just startled me," Lucky said.

"Uh, yeah. That's because *you* startled him."

"Got it." Lucky turned back to Spirit. "Sorry!" she yelled. Spirit spooked again. He ran to the other end of the corral. "Sorry," she whispered this time.

"Just take it slow. Horses can feel what you feel, so if you want him to trust you, you've got to show him the three Cs: calm, confidence—and carrots!" Pru swung off the fence and returned to her chores. "Well, good luck. See you later."

Lucky remembered her groceries. She rummaged through the bag. She didn't have any carrots, but she had potatoes. She pulled out a sad brown potato that looked like a rock. She held it through the fence. Spirit eyed the potato from afar.

"You hungry, bud?" she asked. Spirit did not seem interested. He turned away. "Yeah, I don't like to eat when I'm mad, either."

"Is that a potato?" a girl's voice asked. Lucky turned around to see Abigail trotting toward her on Boomerang.

"Why? Would that be bad?" Lucky asked. She threw the potato behind her.

Abigail slid off Boomerang, looked at Lucky with pity, and pulled a big red apple from her horse's saddlebag.

Boomerang's eyes grew wide, fixating on the apple. His face moved. He tried to grab the apple from Abigail's hand.

"You might want to try something a little less potato-y. Horses are finicky. They have a real sweet tooth," Abigail said, juggling the apple. Boomerang continued to follow it with his eyes, looking dizzy. Abigail tossed the apple to Lucky. Boomerang nickered with disappointment.

"Thanks. That *is* better than a potato," Lucky said.

Abigail nodded and turned back to Boomerang. "I've gotcha covered, buddy. Don't you worry," she cooed at him.

She opened her saddle bag and took out another apple. She took a bite and held the rest out for Boomerang with the palm of her hand open and flat. Boomerang slobbered and scarfed down the apple. Lucky chuckled. It was a little gross, but she felt grateful that Abigail was teaching her. She turned away from Abigail and Boomerang.

"Okay," Lucky said. She laughed nervously. She held out the apple on the palm of her hand, mimicking Abigail. Spirit completely ignored her. "How about this one, Spirit?" She held her hand higher, but Spirit showed no interest in her offering.

"It's okay. You can't rush these things. I spent a whole week singing to Boomerang before he would let me ride him," Abigail said.

"Really?"

"Well, Snips said that Boomerang only really let me ride him so I would stop singing. But I mean, I dunno. Point is, it's just: These things take time." She took the apple from Lucky's hand and rolled it into the corral, halfway between Lucky and Spirit.

"Time? Well, I have plenty of that."

Abigail jumped back on Boomerang and headed into the stables. "See ya later," she said.

Lucky leaned on the fence and watched Spirit come closer to get the apple. "Oh yes!" She yelled in celebration. Spirit spooked and backed away, returning to the other side of the corral. "Oh no. No. Sorry." Lucky remembered that she needed to speak softly. She climbed off the fence, feeling bad.

Spirit pawed at the ground, as if asking for more apples. Maybe they could come to an understanding, after all. "Okay," Lucky said. She didn't have any more apples, but she knew where she could get some.

Lucky ran back to Jim's house. She dropped off the groceries in the kitchen before hurrying to the backyard. She climbed one of the trees and grabbed two apples and then ran back to the Grangers'.

Spirit was standing there, chewing on the fence when she returned. Lucky rolled one of the apples into the corral. Spirit immediately walked to it and gobbled it up. Lucky held out the other apple on her open palm, just as Abigail had taught her. She waited, but Spirit still didn't approach.

Lucky was perplexed. She looked at Abigail, who was grooming Boomerang in the stables. Abigail gestured for her to "just give it time." Then she looked at Pru, who was now training with Chica Linda in the next corral. Pru shook her head at the whole thing.

Lucky closed her fingers around the apple and bit it. She walked away, eating the apple, but looked quickly over her shoulder. Spirit tentatively approached the fence.

But then Chevron and Hendricks appeared, whips and lassos in hand. The horse quickly backed away again.

"Aw, man, how'd he get loose?" Chevron said. Hendricks watched Lucky leave as though he knew the answer.

Lucky ran up the hill to the Prescott house. She didn't turn back.

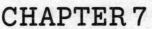

CHAPTER 7

Later, Lucky grabbed two apples from the barrel and loaded them into a bag. Aunt Cora watched from the window but didn't say anything. There was a loud *BANG*. Lucky and Aunt Cora both turned in the direction of the barn. Jim walked out, coughing, in a cloud of smoke. He spotted Lucky and tried to say something to her, but she shrugged him off. He looked frustrated. Aunt Cora rolled her eyes. Lucky packed another couple of apples into her bag and stomped away.

Lucky headed over to the Grangers', something that was quickly becoming a routine. She unpacked her apples, untied Spirit, and rolled three pieces of fruit into the corral. She kept the fourth in her hand and waited for Spirit. He ate the apples in the corral one by one. After the third, he came so close to the fence that Lucky just about burst with excitement. She reached out to try to touch him, but Spirit bolted to the other side of the corral. He wasn't ready. Lucky sat down. She rolled the remaining apple between her hands and sighed, but she did not accept defeat.

Abigail walked over to Lucky from the barn. She held a ukulele in her hands. She sat next to Lucky on the ground. Pru finished her work shortly afterward and joined them. They didn't say anything, but both girls looked at Lucky with something akin to admiration. The sun moved across the sky, making way for clouds to roll in.

Abigail and Pru eventually left as more time passed, but Lucky waited and waited with the apple on her palm. Her eyelids drooped and she fell asleep, still holding the apple.

She did not see Spirit walking to her.

She did not feel him sheltering her from the rain.

She then startled awake for seemingly no reason. By then, rain fell all around her and Spirit's face hovered close to her own as he reached his neck over the fence. Lucky slowly and carefully reached out to him with the remaining apple. He gently took it from her open palm, and the apple disappeared into his mouth. A smile burst onto Lucky's face. Happiness came from deep within her heart. She didn't even feel the rain soaking through her hair and dress. Lucky had finally connected with Spirit.

Abigail and Pru ran from the barn with a blanket over their heads, protecting them from the rain. They beamed. "Yes!" they said together.

"You did it," Abigail added.

They'd watched it all happen. They surrounded Lucky with the blanket. This time, it was Lucky who motioned for them to celebrate quietly. She didn't want them spooking Spirit again.

A chill went up Lucky's spine. She looked over her shoulder and took note of a shadowy figure watching them from the protection of some nearby trees. But she pushed the observation to the back of her head. She didn't want anything ruining the celebration. She felt as if she could do anything.

The next morning, Lucky found Jim and Aunt Cora at the breakfast table. Jim glanced up at Lucky. "Good morning?" he said tentatively.

"Good morning," Lucky replied. "Could you pass me the strawberries?" She gave him a slight smile before heaping eggs and fresh fruit onto her plate.

Lucky was so happy about her breakthrough that she

forgot all about giving Jim the cold shoulder. She didn't even care that there were shells in her eggs. Aunt Cora had clearly been in charge of the food today.

After breakfast, Lucky returned to her room. She kicked her muddy dress from the day before under the bed. She didn't need a lecture from Aunt Cora about it. She pushed aside the dresser and looked at her mother's things more closely. She flipped through the rack of clothes and slid the dresses aside until she found a pair of pants. Lucky figured that these must've been Milagro's riding pants. She pulled them on and stepped in front of the mirror. Though the pants fit, they weren't quite right.... In a moment of inspiration, Lucky tied the purple woven sash Alta Gracia had given her around her waist. She smiled. Perfect.

Lucky snuck out the door and walked through town in her pants. There was a newfound skip in her step. She greeted strangers she saw along the way to Granger's.

"¡Hola! ¡Buenos días!" she said in her best Spanish. She felt as if she was starting to fit in.

She spotted Jim and Al Granger standing on the corner of Main Street, talking. She stayed back where they couldn't see her.

"I said to her, 'No, it's not happening.' I laid down the law. I put my foot down," she overheard Jim say.

"Mmhmm." Al Granger chuckled. "That's good."

68

"I think she got the message."

Both men turned away from the street and focused on one of Hendricks's men pulling down a poster from a nearby wall. "You know, I don't trust those wranglers. Something about that Hendricks is familiar," Al Granger said.

Without waiting to listen, Lucky scurried past them while their backs were turned. There was no one at Granger's today except Spirit. Lucky climbed the corral fence. Spirit looked at her as she jumped in. Lucky took a step toward him, and Spirit took a step back. He huffed, still not completely sure about her. Lucky took another step, and Spirit backed up again. Lucky moved forward again, and Spirit neighed a warning.

"It's okay," Lucky insisted.

She continued to tiptoe toward him and Spirit continued to circle the corral, away from Lucky. Lucky tried to take yet another step. This time, Spirit ran back to where they'd started.

"Easy, boy. Easy," Lucky cooed.

Spirit hesitated, and Lucky took a chance and stepped forward. Spirit reared up and ran even farther away. The exercise continued for a bit as they sized each other up. Then, Lucky began to take another step forward before changing her mind and taking a step backward instead. This confused Spirit. He took a step forward in response.

Lucky gasped. It was another breakthrough!

Lucky took a deep breath and decided to treat this like one of those fancy dances she'd seen at the Prescott mansion parties. She and Spirit circled each other, clockwise and counterclockwise. They went around and around the corral.

Once they were in a groove again, Lucky switched it up and walked backward. Spirit followed. Lucky slowed down and then stopped. Spirit kept walking until they were only a few feet apart. The two stood eye to eye, but Lucky didn't let her excitement get the best of her. She reached into her pocket and pulled out a sugar cube, laying it on her open palm.

"I've got something for you," she said. Spirit sniffed it, and slurped it up into his mouth, leaving her hand full of slobber. "Whoa! Careful with my hand."

She kept her hand held out. Spirit snuffled on it, looking for another treat. When he couldn't find one, he circled around her, sniffing all over. It tickled.

"Hey!" she giggled.

Lucky reached out slowly to touch his neck. Spirit pulled back, but Lucky didn't retreat. She slowly reached out again. This time, Spirit stood still. He let her touch his neck for two seconds before raising his neck out of reach.

"It's okay! It's okay. Easy, boy, easy," she murmured.

Lucky waited a moment. She held out both hands to

show him she meant no harm. Spirit sniffed her hands, then huffed. His breath blew her hair back. She laughed.

"Hey!" She blew back at him jokingly.

Then Lucky walked around to Spirit's side again. She placed her hands on his back. Spirit whinnied and backed away. She stepped closer. He stepped away. They did their little dance several times again, until he moved closer on his own.

Lucky reached for his mane and swung her leg into the air. But then Spirit moved, leaving Lucky to fall on her butt. Without missing a beat, she stood and dusted off her pants.

"Okay, boy, here we go," she said.

She tried again. She grabbed his mane, swung her leg, and...

"Hey there," a small voice said.

Lucky startled and fell to the ground. She looked up to find Snips and Señor Carrots on the other side of the fence. Spirit ran to the other side of the corral, startled by their audience as well.

"Ow." Lucky stood back up and rubbed her butt.

"Whatchu doin'?" Snips said.

"Ugh, Snips. I almost had it!" Lucky said.

"Want some advice?"

"Is it gonna cost me a penny?"

"You just need a boost."

71

Lucky considered for a moment and looked over to the fence. Maybe Snips was right. . . . It seemed easy enough.

Before she knew it, Lucky was straddling the fence close enough to Spirit that he was within touching distance. He eyed her.

"You sure about this?" she said to Snips.

Snips shrugged. "*Pfft*. Easy peasy. Wait a second."

He ran back to pull the carrot Señor Carrots was gnawing out of his mouth. Snips pulled it with such force that it popped into the air and rolled under the corral fence. Spirit eyed the carrot with interest. With Spirit distracted, Lucky made her move and leapt onto the horse's back.

"Easy, boy," she cooed.

Snips opened the gate to get the carrot, and Spirit instantly bolted forward. "Uh-oh." Snips realized the horse was galloping right toward him. He tried to close the gate, but Spirit was too fast.

Spirit ran from the corral. "*Whoooooooaaaaaa!*" Lucky cried.

Snips jumped on Señor Carrots. "Ride like the wind, Señor Carrots!" Señor Carrots ran behind them as fast as his little burro legs could take him. It wasn't very fast, though, and Spirit and Lucky left them in the dust.

Lucky held on to Spirit's mane tightly, jostling around like a rag doll on his back.

They zoomed by Pru, who was behind the barn, watering Chica Linda. Pru gasped. "Watch it! *Ooh*, that's not good," she said.

"Whoa! Please! Whoa!" Lucky tightened her legs around Spirit and held on for her life.

But Spirit only picked up speed. Lucky was half terrified, but also oddly exhilarated.

"Slow down a little. Please?" She tried to negotiate with him. Spirit slowed, raised his legs, and tried to buck her off. "Whoa. That's not what I meant. Whoa! Careful."

Spirit picked up the pace again. He made a beeline for the edge of town. She could see Abigail up ahead—practicing her barrel-racing moves, pivoting Boomerang around two barrels.

"Wow. You really went for it," Abigail yelled, mid-roll. "Good for you."

"How do you *stoooooop*?" Lucky yelled back as they tore past her.

Pru was racing behind Lucky now. She zoomed past Abigail. "She needs help. Come on!" she said.

"She looks like fun." Abigail smiled. She and Boomerang took off running.

Spirit raced toward the canyon. Lucky leaned into him, holding her body as close to his as possible and trying to get her bearings. Spirit jumped over a rock. This jostled Lucky, nearly sending her flying. She clung tighter to him, keeping her head and body low.

"Whoa! Whoa!" she repeated. Spirit glanced back at her with a look of surprise, as if he'd forgotten she was there.

Lucky could hear Pru and Abigail and the trot of their horses behind them, but their voices sounded far away.

"Yah! Come on, Boomerang!" Abigail encouraged.

"Yah! Come on, let's go, girl! Go, go, go!" Pru urged Chica Linda.

The path ahead split into two. Spirit veered onto the narrow cliff edge. "Hold on! Wait, we have to turn back," Lucky pleaded with him.

Pru and Abigail stayed on the wider path and ran parallel to Lucky through the canyon. Abigail eyed the drop below. Then she looked at Lucky. Spirit brushed against the canyon, and Lucky almost tumbled off, sending rocks down into the pass.

"Good thing her name's Lucky!" Abigail said.

"Well, is her middle name Irony?" Pru asked. "Lucky, sit up and hold on with your legs."

Lucky tried to get traction by squeezing her thighs even harder. Spirit continued to weave along the curves of the canyon.

"Or just hang on, and whatever you do, don't look down," Abigail yelled.

74

More rocks flew over the edge. Lucky couldn't help it. She glanced down and saw the deadly drop below. "Too late," she said.

She took a deep breath, trying to recover from her shock. Pru and Abigail looked straight ahead, horror-struck. Lucky followed their eyes and saw that the drop wasn't the worst of it. There was a gap in the path ahead.

"Just slow down, please! Spirit, you have to stop!" But Spirit plowed ahead. They were going so fast that her words were lost in the wind as they cut through the canyon.

Pru and Abigail veered across a narrow canyon "bridge" connecting the two paths. Lucky watched them over her shoulder. They fell in line right behind Lucky. Abigail looked as if she was trying hard not to glance down. She pushed Boomerang to go faster.

"You're getting so many carrots later, bud," she said to him. They began to close the gap on Spirit.

"Hi," Lucky said to the two girls. She felt some of the tension ease out of her.

"Let's do the two-hand pickup," Abigail said to Pru.

"The what now?" Pru said.

"Just grab a hand on the count of two," Abigail said. "One."

"Two!" both girls said. Chica Linda and Boomerang flanked Spirit. The girls lunged for Lucky, but she was just

75

out of reach. The path was evaporating quickly. They were almost out of runway.

"Jump!" the girls yelled at Lucky.

Lucky reached back and leapt off Spirit as Abigail's left hand swung her toward Pru, who grabbed her just as Boomerang and Chica Linda screeched to a halt. Lucky landed hard behind Pru on the back of Chica Linda. More rocks tumbled off the edge.

Spirit continued to run toward the gap, picking up another wind of speed and stretching into a stunning leap over the chasm. He landed on the other side and bolted around the corner.

Lucky watched him disappear from view. She caught her breath, finally feeling pure exhilaration. That had been some ride.

"Wow. I just rode a horse! I almost died, but I just rode a horse!" she said.

"Around here we call that *hanging on for dear life*," Pru said over her shoulder.

Abigail chuckled. "Hey, but it's a start! You're a natural," she said.

"Don't encourage her," Pru muttered. They retraced their steps out from the canyon.

Jim and Al Granger were headed their way on their own horses. "There they are!" Al Granger said.

Lucky jumped off Chica Linda. Jim rushed to her in a panic. He pulled on the reins of his horse and stopped in front of her before leaping to the ground. "Lucky! Whoa! Lucky, are you okay?" Lucky nodded, still catching her breath. A look of relief washed over Jim as he inspected her. "Fingers. Toes. Face. Everything is okay. Okay. You're okay. I'm okay," he said. "She's okay, Al. Whole girl here," he called back.

"I can see that," Al said. He chuckled.

"But how did you know?" Pru asked her dad. Snips and Señor Carrots suddenly careened around the corner, nearly tipping over.

"Did you see me?" Lucky asked Jim excitedly. "It was amazing. We were going so fast and it was a little scary, but mostly exciting and then—"

Jim interrupted her. "Lucky, you are lucky you didn't get yourself killed." His head dropped. Lucky could see the anger surfacing.

"I know, but I was going to ride him in the corral and then...," she said.

"Well, there was this gust of wind and the gate flew open, which I had nothing to do with! And then...Lucky fell onto the horse and it took off," Snips chimed in. He was still trying to save her.

"Home. Now. You shouldn't have been anywhere near

that horse," he said to Lucky, ignoring Snips. Lucky was taken aback by his abruptness. She felt completely deflated now.

"Come on, troublemakers," Al Granger said. Pru, Abigail, Snips, and their herd of four-legged conspirators followed.

CHAPTER 8

Lucky wanted to run straight to her
room, but Jim wouldn't let up. Aunt Cora was standing in
the hallway with a box in her hands when they arrived back
at the house. She took one look at them and then shook her
head and retreated. Jim slammed the front door.

"I asked for one thing. One," he said. He held up his
forefinger for emphasis.

"It was an accident," Lucky said.

"You don't listen."

"But..."

"You don't listen. That horse doesn't belong to you."

"He doesn't belong to those"—what was that word Al

Granger had used?—"wranglers. They're mistreating him, and you don't even care!"

"This isn't the city. Around here we have different rules."

"Well, you should change your rules, and by the way, you can't just come back into my life and tell me what to do." Lucky started up the stairs.

"You're going back to your grandfather's. You'll be safer there."

Lucky stopped mid-step. "What? That's not fair!" she said, her back still to him.

"I'm getting you and your aunt on the next train," he continued. Her heart was breaking right then and there, but she wouldn't give him the satisfaction of telling him.

She turned around and looked him right in the eye. "I thought Prescotts never give up, but you're giving up on me. Again," she growled.

"I'm trying to keep you safe," Jim pleaded, slumping into the stairs a little. Fear rose into his eyes. Maybe his heart was breaking, too.

"Sorry to be such a burden!" Lucky said. She ran to her room and slammed the door.

She leaned against the door, breathing heavily. Once she calmed some, she could hear Aunt Cora talking.

"Well, just be thankful nothing's on fire," she said to Jim.

Lucky didn't know what to do. She paced up and down

her room. She paused and threw open the window. She needed air. Air blew in, swirling around her. She closed her eyes, allowing the breeze to calm her. She heard the faintest whinny in the distance. Could that be Spirit? Her eyes flew open.

Lucky leaned out the window and scanned the horizon in the direction of the canyon. The breeze picked up and she didn't hear Spirit anymore. She did hear the *tic-tic-tic* of the zoetrope, though. Lucky glanced at her mother's dressing room and, for the first time, noticed a glimmer of red peeking out from the closet. She walked over to it and parted the hanging clothes. On the floor sat a pair of red leather riding boots with intricate patterns along the sides.

Lucky sat on the floor and pulled the boots on. She looked at herself in the mirror, now in her mother's pants, boots, and sash. She stood there, trying not to listen to the conversation downstairs, but found that it was impossible to drown out.

"What did you expect? You never came to visit her," Aunt Cora said in a voice louder than her usual composure allowed.

"She's just not safe here. She was doing so well with you; I didn't want to complicate things," Jim defended himself. "I couldn't keep her mother safe. How was I supposed to keep her safe?"

"What happened to Milagro was an accident. You said yourself she'd done that trick a hundred times before with her eyes closed. Jim, I've done everything I can for Lucky. What she needs now more than anything is her father. She needs you. Sometimes you have to take a risk."

"I did that already and that didn't work out. I couldn't bear it if anything happened to her. Cora, I don't know what I'm doing. She's so reckless."

"Well, the apple doesn't fall far from the tree."

Lucky heard the whinny in the distance again. She ran to the window. It was growing too dark and foggy now to see anything. Without a moment's hesitation, she climbed through the window to the tree to see if the view was better. When it wasn't, she shimmied down the tree, dropped to the ground, and stood up. Lucky plucked an armful of apples from the low-hanging branches and tied them into her sash. She decided to follow the sound.

Lucky ran, slowing for a moment as she drew farther away to look back at Jim's house. Before she could second-guess herself, she pushed onward. She snuck past the sleeping cowboy and his llama at the train depot. She walked along the metal train tracks, listening carefully for the sound of Spirit. She heard the hoot of an owl as she neared a bridge that seemed to connect Miradero to a wooded area. Lucky was starting to learn that Miradero was full of surprises. It wasn't all dusty town and desert.

A yellowish light moved toward her through the fog, like a train coming down the tracks and headed straight for her!

Lucky panicked before she realized she didn't hear a whistle and couldn't feel the telltale rumble of a train. Then, the light burst into a sparkle of fireflies. The fireflies danced all around her, and Lucky drew a breath in amazement. She laughed softly, watching them flutter back into the wooded area, as if lighting the way for her.

She heard the whinny again. This time it sounded closer. She followed the sound and the tiny dancing lights, not noticing that she was stepping away from the train tracks and pushing through foliage that grew thicker as she pressed on. The moonlight occasionally cut through the fog and helped light her way. Eventually, Lucky came upon a large rock blocking the path. She hoisted herself up on it, slid down the other side, and landed on her feet.

"Whoa!" she said.

A symphony of mysterious sounds grew from all directions. There was the *whoosh* of the wind, the singing of insects, and the shuffle of larger animals moving about. A howl echoed from somewhere within the abyss. Lucky turned and gasped. She also heard the quickening of her own heart. Was that the silhouette of a coyote atop a mound of boulders? Her eyes adjusted in the fog again. They revealed that it was merely a rock formation. She let out a sigh of relief, climbed the rock, and peered over the top. On the other side, she saw a beautiful, endless field of fireflies. She jumped down.

The fireflies fluttered around Lucky. Their golden light blinked on and off. The fog cleared above them, and the sky overhead began to twinkle, too. The stars looked close enough to touch. Lucky reached up. The little lights of the fireflies slowly spiraled upward, as if they, too, wanted to touch the stars. The little lights magically blended into the sky.

"Wow," Lucky said.

Lucky suddenly heard footsteps coming closer and closer. Something large was pushing through the fog. She held her breath. The dark figure revealed itself....

"Spirit!" Lucky said with relief and pure joy.

She rushed to him, and Spirit chuffed. Lucky remembered to take it slow. She inhaled for a beat and took a step back. Spirit came to her. Then she slowly reached out and touched his snout. He nicked at her playfully and nudged her hand. Lucky put both her arms around him in a hug. Spirit didn't move away this time. He rested his head on her shoulder and nuzzled her side. Lucky wondered if this was his way of hugging her back or if he was actually just digging around for apples.

Whatever it was, it tickled. Lucky laughed and pulled out an apple. "Hey, boy, I knew I'd see you again."

She watched him gobble it up. His ears perked up. There was more rustling in the fog. Something else approached. Lucky held her breath once more.

Out from the fog stepped two more horses.

There was more rustling, then more horses. Lucky and Spirit were now surrounded by a circle of wild horses. "Wow. This must be your family," Lucky whispered.

The horses whinnied but kept their distance. They looked to Spirit, their leader, and exchanged neighs with him as if asking about Lucky. "It's okay," she said. She rolled more apples into the circle. "Oh, I hope I brought enough."

One of the horses stepped forward to take an apple. This appeared to give the others courage. They moved in closer, taking the offerings. A foal stepped from behind his mother's haunches, peeking at Lucky with curious eyes. She held up another apple for the small horse, who did not wait for her to roll it. He trotted right up to her and ate it from her hand. Lucky was surprised and humbled.

"Hello, Little Brave One," she said. The foal trotted back to his mother, his head held high.

Spirit's ears perked up again. But something in his entire

demeanor changed this time. His breathing picked up. "What's wrong?" Lucky whispered.

Suddenly, Hendricks and a couple of his wranglers emerged from the fog on horses, lassos drawn. The herd reared up in panic, circling even closer to Lucky. The wranglers charged. Lucky stood hidden in the middle of the horses, trying not to get trampled.

"All right, boys, let's round 'em up," Hendricks said. "I told you we'd get the rest of 'em. Get all of 'em. Every single one." Lucky heard a series of yahs, whoo-hoos, and hee-yahs! The wranglers broke the herd apart and began tying them.

They pulled the mama horse to the ground. Little Brave One stood nearby, shaking. Spirit ran and knocked Walrus from his horse, making him drop the rope he was holding.

"We should've just robbed a bank," Walrus said.

Spirit turned to face Hendricks.

"The stallion's mine," Hendricks growled.

Lucky thankfully hadn't been noticed by the wranglers, but she didn't know what to do. She needed help. With the horses and the men distracted, she ran and ran until she tripped over the fog-covered train tracks. Catching her breath, Lucky pulled herself up and stepped back just in time. The fog dispersed to reveal a steam engine barreling toward her. It slowed to a halt and the ramp to the attached train car dropped with a thump. Before she could react, Lucky heard Hendricks and his men arrive behind her with Spirit's herd in tow.

"Hurry it up. Come on. Load 'em up!" Hendricks ordered. "Have a nice ride, ladies. Go on, get in there."

Chevron pulled the mama horse up the ramp. Meanwhile, Hendricks kicked Little Brave One down to his knees. The foal struggled to stand back up and climb the ramp.

"You can't do this!" Lucky yelled. "Those horses aren't yours!"

"Ain't no first class on this train. These horses are none of your business. But thank you for leading me straight to them," Hendricks said.

His men continued to drive the herd up the ramp and into the car. Spirit, meanwhile, continued to fight. He knocked Horseshoe and Chevron off their horses. Then he kicked at the ground, ready to charge Hendricks.

"I got you now, boy," he growled.

Lucky threw her last apple straight at Hendricks's head.

"Ow!" he cried.

It was just the distraction Spirit needed. He charged straight at Hendricks. Hendricks flew off his horse and landed on the dirt with a thud. He looked up at Spirit with vengeful eyes as the train ramp closed shut. The whistle blew.

"Hendricks! We gotta go before they find out their train

is missing. We can't miss the six AM boat," Chevron said. Chevron and Walrus tried to pull their leader to his feet.

"Get off me," he said, shaking them off him. "Change of plan, boys. That one stays here."

The crew jumped on the moving train as it picked up steam. Without missing a beat, Spirit followed, desperately trying to keep up with his herd. Lucky ran, too, but her two legs were no match for his four. Instead, she turned around and ran in the opposite direction.

She saw Miradero getting closer, but it wasn't close enough. Lucky had to stop to catch her breath. She dropped to her knees, feeling defeated. Then she heard something behind her.

She looked over her shoulder. Spirit had returned. He dropped on his front legs next to Lucky. She looked in his eyes. In their depths, he told her all the things he had no words for. He had never submitted to anyone. But he needed her. His herd needed her.

"Okay, but we can't do this alone," she said to him, pointing in the direction of town. Spirit whinnied. Lucky climbed on his back. "All right, boy, let's get some help." They headed down the hill, toward Main Street.

CHAPTER 9

Lucky saw a light on in the barn at Granger's. She jumped off Spirit and burst through the doors. Pru jolted upright and Chica Linda coughed out a mouthful of hay, as if choking. They side-eyed Lucky simultaneously.

"Pru, I need your help," Lucky said. She explained what had happened.

Once she had heard everything, Pru pulled a map from a cabinet and rolled it out over a nearby saddle. The girls knelt to look at it. Chica Linda watched skeptically over their shoulders.

"So, you're saying you want us to skip town without a trace, ride all night to stop a speeding train, take down a band of dirty old thieves, and release a herd of wild horses?" Pru asked. She calmly handed Lucky a canteen of water.

Lucky chugged it. "*Yeaaa*—maybe," she said. "If we don't try, Spirit's herd is gone forever."

"Let me show you exactly how impossible it is. Hendricks and his men are headed for a boat up here at the docks on a speeding train." Pru pointed at one spot on the map. Then she pointed at a different spot, way farther down. "We're down here with the horses. It's too far."

Lucky listened to Spirit whinnying outside. She couldn't give up that easily. She looked at the map and racked her brain. She focused on the one thing on the map she knew about as a Prescott: the trains. "What if we take the shortcut over this big pointy thingy?" She traced her finger over a mountain on the map to the Water Depot, where two train lines met and turned into one.

"That big pointy thing is Heck Mountain. It's impossible to cross on horseback. That's a full day and most of a night's ride. Even if by some miracle we did make it, how are we supposed to get the horses off of a moving train?"

Lucky thought back to her math homework. "If a train traveling at twenty-five miles an hour has to stop every one hundred miles..." She spoke louder as she continued. "Aunt Cora was right! I *do* need to know this!"

"Uh, what now?"

Lucky pointed to the Water Depot on the map again. "A steam engine has to stop to refill water along the way. If we cut over the mountain, we can beat the train to this Water Depot at"—she counted on her fingers—"noon tomorrow." She looked at the map again. "Whoa, what's the Ridge of Regret?"

Pru stood up. Chica Linda snorted and turned back to her hay, flicking Lucky with her tail. "You don't want to know," Pru said.

A ukulele strummed ominously from somewhere in the barn. They turned to see the outline of a figure atop a horse.

Abigail rode slowly from the darkness with her ukulele in hand. "From what I hear, there's a lotta dangers lurking around those parts. Dangers that only those with good fortune return from," she said.

"Return from?" Lucky replied. She and Pru looked at each other.

"I've heard tales. The most treacherous and merciless creatures hiding in the shadows. Creatures you wouldn't believe." Abigail hopped off Boomerang. She grabbed the lantern and began to narrate a story with a series of increasingly elaborate shadow puppets. "There's a moose, and he's a'waiting, but he doesn't know what he's a'waiting for. And they say at the bottom of a bridge is a shifty fox. Who's just sitting there being...shifty! And then there's a possum that

91

just hangs out lighting matches. Ha ha ha!" Abigail looked at the shadows on the wall. Scared of her own creation, she ran behind the other girls for protection, knocking the lantern over. Everyone, including the horses, stared at Abigail.

"Abigail!" Pru chided her, picking up the lantern and then turning to Lucky. "I think what Abigail is *trying* to say is it's way too dangerous."

"Well, I have to try. Spirit and I will be fine on our own," Lucky said. She was clearly afraid, but she'd never let fear stop her before. She squared her shoulders and walked from the barn.

"She don't listen," Pru said to Abigail. She sighed and picked up the saddle and the map.

"You know, Pru," Abigail said, "any other girl would never be able to save those poor, innocent horses."

"Uh-oh. I smell rule-breaking," a small voice chimed in.

Snips rounded the barn door atop Señor Carrots. Abigail grinned mischievously. She reached for her lasso hanging on Boomerang's saddle. She popped her gum and blew a bubble. Then she waved goodbye to her little brother.

"Hey, Lucky! Wait up!" Abigail called. "Wait for us."

"Uh, Lucky! Lucky!" Pru called.

Despite her bravado, Lucky was relieved to see Abigail,

Pru, Boomerang, and Chica Linda approaching. She was glad that she didn't have to have this particular adventure alone. Once the newcomers reached them, Spirit tried to pull forward, eager to press on. Boomerang licked him. Spirit huffed. He did not seem pleased. It relieved some of the tension, nonetheless.

The group rode toward the edge of the bridge. They walked down the bridge in a line, Pru in front, Lucky in the middle, and Abigail pulling up the rear.

"I still think this is a terrible idea," Pru declared.

"But...," Abigail prompted.

"I don't have a *but*. It's just a terrible idea," Pru continued. Abigail folded her arms. She gave Pru a hard stare. "*But* this is Miradero. Out here, we stick together." Pru sighed.

"Thanks, guys," Lucky said.

"We better hurry up if we want to make it to the Water Depot before noon tomorrow." Pru pointed at the mountain in the far distance. "You can thank us after we make it over that big pointy thing," she said.

"Heck Mountain!" Abigail clarified.

Lucky tapped Spirit, determined to make it in time. Spirit hustled down the bridge past Pru and Chica Linda. Lucky flailed, almost falling off. "Whoa! Easy, boy," she called.

"In case you don't want to get thrown, keep your heels

down, shoulders back, eyes where you want him to go," Pru said, following Lucky to the other side of the bridge.

Abigail caught up. She rode up next to Lucky. "Yeah, but, like, not so..." She copied Lucky's stiff posture; she looked like a mannequin. "You're liable to cramp," she explained.

Lucky was confused by the conflicting advice. She just wanted to press forward. "I know. I know." She brushed off both girls. But she didn't know. This was only her second time on a horse. Lucky struggled to stay atop Spirit. "Hold on, Spirit, careful!"

"When you trust yourself, your horse will, too. He'll know exactly what you're thinking, even before you do. Then you'll be *joined up*," Pru said.

"What's that?" Lucky asked.

"'Joined Up'?" Abigail gasped. "That's my favorite trail song!"

"Oh no." Pru sighed. She didn't get to elaborate, because Abigail was already strumming her ukulele.

Abigail sang as they traversed desert and forest, until they came upon the mountain.

The sun broke over the horizon just as Lucky, Pru, and Abigail rode into the canyon. Lucky still felt uneasy riding Spirit. She focused all her energy on staying upright.

"We heard all about the time you 'liberated' a monkey

from the zoo," Abigail said, braiding Boomerang's mane. Lucky smiled and relaxed a little.

"The birthday that you flooded—" Pru said.

"Or that time you accidentally locked the math tutor in the closet and couldn't get him out," Abigail interrupted.

"Or when Lucky sicced a squirrel on her grandfather!" Pru added. The three girls burst into laughter.

"I did get into trouble for that one." Lucky thought about how they knew all of this. "Jim really talks about me that much?"

Pru and Abigail nodded. "Sometimes my dad pretends he has to go to the bathroom just to get your dad to stop talking about you," Pru said.

The girls were now deep in the canyon. Lucky looked on with awe. Large, moose-shaped rocks loomed overhead. "See, I told you there was a moose a'waiting," Abigail said. Lucky and Pru looked at each other and burst into laughter again.

Pru grabbed the map from her saddle and studied it. She held the paper up to show the other girls. "Here it is. We cross this bridge, and it's a straight shot up the mountain to the Water Depot," she said.

And so they followed the map. They rounded a bend in the trail and came upon another bridge. This one was a threadbare suspension bridge. It swayed back and forth, though there appeared to be no breeze.

"Is it supposed to move that much?" Lucky asked nervously.

"It's fine. Suspension bridges are built to support incredible weights," Pru said. Chica Linda placed a single hoof on one of the slats and the piece of wood dislodged and plummeted into the canyon.

Lucky held her breath. There was a distant clatter. She looked over the edge and gulped. *"Oooof."* Lucky's shoulders slumped. She looked at Spirit, then at Abigail and Pru.

"Now what?" Abigail asked.

"Now we go back home is what," Pru said.

"And just give up?" Lucky said. Lucky took Spirit to the edge of the canyon and looked at the gaping space below. She looked around for any other possible routes.

"I'm sorry, Lucky," Pru insisted.

"No. Give me a minute. I'll figure out a different way," Lucky pleaded.

"Take your time. Boomerang and I will just wait over here!" Abigail bellowed. Lucky and Pru looked over. Abigail was waving from the other side of the bridge.

"How did she..." Pru seemed flabbergasted.

"What? The great Pru Granger can't handle a little jump?" Abigail taunted playfully.

"I can, but *we* can't!" Pru gestured toward Lucky.

Lucky looked back and forth between Abigail and Pru. "What? Sure *we* can. I can do it. I can do it. I think." They approached the start of the bridge.

"Okay, it's on. Let's go show them how it's done, Chica," Pru said in her competitive voice. She turned to Lucky. "When you get to the edge where there's a big gap in the slats, lean in and trust him. Spirit will do the rest. He'll get you on the platform. Just don't pull back. You ready?" Pru lined Chica Linda up to cross.

"You mean now?" Lucky wasn't so sure anymore.

"What you need—" Pru didn't get to finish.

Spirit flared his nostrils and charged forward. "*Ahhhhh!*" Lucky yelled.

"I think you better just hold on!" Pru said. Pru and Chica Linda broke into a gallop alongside them and pulled ahead. They were almost on the other side of the bridge. Pru leaned forward and relaxed her grip, letting Chica Linda take over. Chica Linda vaulted up, up, up and landed on the other side in a cloud of dust.

"Steady. Head up, look ahead. Not down. Never look down," Pru coached.

But Lucky couldn't help herself—she looked down into the chasm and gulped as Spirit vaulted into the air. Lucky tensed with fear. She grabbed Spirit tight around the neck. The distraction tripped Spirit up. He struggled to get his footing on the platform and slipped. The two skidded down the side of the canyon, kicking up plumes of dust.

"Lucky!" Pru and Abigail called. Lucky closed her eyes and held on for dear life. Her hold broke and she fell from Spirit's back. She tumbled down, down, down.

When she finally slowed to a stop, Lucky opened her eyes. She was on the ground. She could barely see her feet in front of her with all the dust hanging in the air. She coughed, choking slightly. There was no sign of Spirit. She panicked.

"Spirit! Spirit. Where are you?" She coughed again and gasped for air.

Lucky pulled herself to her feet. She covered her nose and mouth with her arm and put her other hand out to feel her way around. The dust slowly settled. When it did, Lucky spotted Spirit on the ground up ahead. She ran to his side.

"Spirit! Spirit," she cried.

There were scrapes on his legs and sides and he was breathing as hard as she was. She remembered Pru's advice about Spirit feeling what she felt. She counted to ten and tried to calm herself. She slowed her breathing and put her hand on his side so that he could feel her slowing pulse.

"It's okay," she cooed.

As she calmed, so did Spirit. After a moment, he tested his weight on his legs. He stood up and shook off the fall. Everything seemed to be working. Spirit nuzzled Lucky.

She felt so relieved that she buried her face in his neck without thinking.

Once she realized what she was doing, she jerked her body back. "I'm sorry, boy. I should've trusted you."

Chica Linda and Boomerang whinnied from somewhere above them. Spirit perked up his ears and called back to the other horses. Lucky squinted up toward the top of the canyon. A small ray of light cut down to them. She couldn't see the horses or her friends, but she could hear them.

"Abigail? Pru?" Lucky yelled.

"Are you dead?" Abigail called down.

"A little." Lucky laughed. She quickly stopped because everything hurt. "I could really use that possum lighting matches."

"There might be a way out farther down—just follow our voices," Pru said.

"Good idea. I'll sing you a song!" Abigail said. "*Row, row, row your boat, gently down the stream,*" she belted out.

"Atta boy, Spirit," Lucky cooed. She touched his nose gently. He followed her, down the canyon, one step at a time. Lucky remounted. She spotted a path back to the top filled with boulders. "Come on, Spirit," she urged.

Spirit and Lucky trudged forward. He hopped over the first boulder. Lucky nervously gripped his neck again, causing him to scramble.

"*Row, row, row your boat gently down the stream,*" Abigail continued singing.

"Intermission," Pru said to Abigail. She redirected her attention to Lucky. "Just trust him and move with him. Breathe. You guys can do this."

"You gotta loosen up. I said, *loosen,*" Abigail reminded her.

Lucky took a deep breath and tried to follow all the advice that her friends had given her. She let Spirit take over. He got his footing back. "Okay, we've got this," she said. Lucky and Spirit struggled over the rocks, climbing farther and farther up. They could see their friends now.

"C'mon, Abigail. Let's clear a path," Pru said.

Pru guided Chica Linda like she did in the ring. Chica Linda kicked the rocks out of the way with her fancy footwork, clearing the path for Lucky and Spirit. Abigail lassoed the big rocks, putting the lariat in Boomerang's mouth. He walked backward and pulled the obstacles out of the way.

The girls watched nervously as Lucky and Spirit moved in sync now. "Easy there. Easy, boy," Lucky said to him.

"Yes! You got it!" Pru cheered. Lucky and Spirit made the last jump up onto the ledge.

"We never doubted you!" Abigail said. "I thought she was a goner," she whispered to Pru under her breath.

"I told you we'd find a different way." Lucky broke into a grin. The horses whinnied and snorted in celebration.

"I'd call that different, all right," Abigail laughed.

"Yeah, but now we're too far down the canyon and don't have time to backtrack," Pru said.

Lucky trotted past the girls with newfound confidence. "Let's go up farther so that we can get a better idea of where we are," she said.

The temperature dropped significantly as they rode up the mountain. They seemed to be walking through clouds. Spirit and Lucky stopped at the precipice. Before them lay an extremely narrow ridge with a steep drop on either side. It appeared to be the only way across. "I'm guessing this is the Ridge of Regret."

Pru nodded quickly. Chica Linda pawed at the ground. Part of the earth crumbled into the clouds below them. "Chica Linda! Careful, girl!" she said.

The wind whipped through the sky. Abigail shook her head from side to side. "Ooh, I regret it already," she said.

"This would be a good time for advice," Lucky said.

But the girls didn't reply. Lucky turned to them. Abigail and Pru were looking at the river below with horror. Lucky second-guessed herself. If she couldn't safely cross a bridge, then maybe this was not something they should even consider.

As if he could sense her hesitation, Spirit neighed and pulled onto the ridge.

"Lucky!" Abigail and Pru warned.

Lucky felt panic and clenched her fists. Spirit neighed softly and looked back at Lucky almost reassuringly. She took a deep breath and remembered to trust him. She relaxed her posture, and Spirit moved forward into an easy gait. Lucky closed her eyes to let Spirit lead.

A song came to her mind. She couldn't remember where she'd heard it. Maybe it was another one of the songs her mother had sung to her as a baby.

Maybe she sang it to distract herself. Maybe she was singing to Spirit. Either way, Spirit took it one step at a time and moved carefully across the ridge.

Pru and Abigail shared a look. Abigail pulled out her ukulele. "Here we go," Abigail said. She strummed along to the song, following Lucky onto the ridge.

Pru looked at Chica Linda and the other girls. She took a deep breath and stepped onto the ridge, too. She harmonized with Lucky.

The three girls hummed and harmonized. They crept across the ridge. Rocks and pebbles fell from under their horses' hooves. Boomerang lost his footing a bit but managed to rebalance.

Lucky finally felt Spirit's hooves land on solid ground. She opened her eyes. The horse neighed at her and she laid her head on him. They shared a moment. "Thank you, Spirit," she said.

"Oh my gosh," Pru said, now at their side.

Abigail approached, too. She slid off Boomerang and rolled onto the ground. "Oh, I love you, ground! So solid! So supportive! So reassuring!"

Spirit touched noses with Boomerang and Chica Linda, as if checking to make sure they were okay. Pru looked at Lucky meaningfully. "Only Lucky Prescott would finally join up with her horse on the Ridge of Regret," she said.

"I couldn't have done it without you." Lucky smiled.

Abigail pointed. "Look! The Water Depot. We made it," she said.

"We can camp at the overlook. When the train comes tomorrow at noon, we'll see it for miles," Pru said.

The girls and their horses headed toward the Water Depot. Lucky slid off Spirit. She struggled to get her land legs back. "I'm walking the rest of the way," Lucky said, rubbing at her backside.

"You guys are pretty good singers. We should start a band!" Abigail said. Pru rolled her eyes.

CHAPTER 10

The overlook was a magnificent rock overhang that jutted out of the mountain in the shape of the letter *C*. Lucky had never seen anything like it. She hadn't had much time to appreciate the beauty of the landscape around them until now.

The Water Depot was very close. Abigail and Pru gathered fallen brush and started a campfire to warm them up.

"We're going to get your family back. I promise," Lucky whispered to Spirit.

The girls sat down in a circle around the fire. The fire blazed, lighting their faces. "Tomorrow we face our destiny, but tonight, we *feast*!" Abigail brandished a stick. She pulled a stack of marshmallows from her saddlebag.

"Woo! Yes! I'm starving," Pru said.

"I always prepare for the unexpected. We'll need the strength of a thousand marshmallows if we're gonna take down those rustlers." Abigail passed out sticks and they speared their marshmallows. They lay the sticks on the rocks by the fire to toast their dinner. There was a glimmer of something in Abigail's eyes. She picked up her lasso. With one swing, she roped Lucky and pulled her closer. "Pru, look! I caught a wild one!" she said.

Lucky chuckled and tried to get herself loose. She looked at the two girls.

"What?" Pru said.

"Do I have marshmallow face?" Abigail asked, stuffing the marshmallows into her mouth.

Lucky chuckled again, the rope now tangled even more around her. "No. Well, yes. But that's not it. We crossed the Ridge of Regret. *Us.*"

"Yeah, we did the impossible." Pru nodded and joined in the laughter. She tried to help Lucky but got snagged in the tangle as well.

"That was wild." Abigail cracked up. She mumbled with her mouth full. "We made bad choices."

All three giggled hysterically now. "And tomorrow we're going to take on a bunch of dangerous wranglers. We might get killed!" Lucky said between breaths.

"It's not funny!" Pru said, laughing even harder.

"Stop, you're making my stomach hurt," Lucky cried.

Pru tried to quiet down, but this just made them erupt into more laughter. Boomerang shoved his head into the bag of marshmallows, trying to be sneaky.

"Boomerang P. Stubbles! Get out of there!" Abigail said to him.

He pulled his head out, guilty-faced with a marshmallow stuck to his cheek. Chica Linda shook her head from side to side. She plucked the marshmallow off him and munched it happily. The two horses watched Spirit patrolling the area and then joined him.

The girls lay back near the fire. "You can see all the stars in the universe from here," Pru said.

"I wonder if they can see us," Lucky said.

"Course they can. Stars sleep during the day and gaze at night," Abigail said. She popped up and dug into her saddle-bag. "I almost forgot. I made us these." She gave them each a bracelet made of twine and things she'd found along the trail: rock fragments and pieces of flat bark stenciled with each of their initials.

"Aw, Abigail," Lucky said.

"When did you have time?" Pru slipped the bracelet on. The girls turned their wrists, admiring them. They jingled.

"There's always time for friendship-based crafting," she

said. "P.A....No, wait." Abigail scooted around so that her *A* was right side up and in line with Pru and Lucky's wrists. "Pru, Abigail, and Lucky. We're PALs!"

"I'm never going to take this off," Pru said quietly.

"Pru! You big softie. I knew you liked me!" Abigail teased. She threw her arms around her.

Pru stiffened and tried to free herself. "Okay. Cut it out. Cut it out! You're getting marshmallow on me."

"Never. Never." Abigail laughed and hugged her tighter. Lucky smiled. The three horses returned to the campfire with the girls.

This was their herd.

Lucky felt as if she finally had friends for the first time in her life. She started to sing Abigail's trail song.

Pru relaxed her posture and joined Lucky.

Abigail dived for her ukulele. She strummed along to the song. The three girls finished—their voices cracking when they hit the high note at the end.

They collapsed into giggles again.

Abigail jolted up. "Hush! Do you hear that? It's the shifty fox!" she said. Pru and Lucky laughed even harder. They spent the rest of the night giggling by the fireside until they dozed off, one by one.

Lucky woke up just as the sun was becoming an outline of red on the horizon. She shook the other girls awake. They packed up and threw dirt on the embers of their campfire. Then they rode to the edge of the canyon and looked down at the train tracks.

"All right, remember the plan. First, we're gonna get to the Water Depot," Pru said.

Abigail tried on her best announcer voice. "Then we're going to bring the reign of righteous retribution...." The train chugged along in the distance.

"Yah!" Lucky said. The girls sprang into action.

"Yah! Let's go! Woo!" Abigail said.

"Come on, Chica! Faster," Pru urged her horse.

The six of them raced down the hill, behind the train. Lucky and Spirit galloped toward the engine. Spirit was gaining on it. Lucky could see that it was Hendricks driving the train.

Lucky tried to stand on Spirit's back. She needed a miracle. She looked down at her mother's red boots and knew that she had one. Milagro was watching over her. She pushed herself up. She was standing on Spirit's back now! She leapt onto the train as if she were one of Las Caballeras performing a trick.

"Huh?" Hendricks was looking at them now. He opened his eyes wide with disbelief. "Hey, little..."

Lucky jump-kicked him, raising her leg like she'd learned in one of her ballet classes and knocking him out. Then she kicked the brake lever. The train came to a screeching halt.

"Ha ha! Ha!" Lucky said. She jumped on top of the engine and ran along the roof of the train to the livestock car. She leapt over the divide, outrunning three wranglers. "On three! One!" she yelled at the girls, who had joined her on the train. She kicked Walrus in the face. He screamed as he fell off the train. "Two!" She kicked Horseshoe. "Three." Pru and Abigail opened the door of the livestock car, freeing the herd.

"Woo!" They burst into celebration. The horses whinnied.

"I'll show you...," Lucky mumbled in her sleep. Spirit whinnied with anguish in the distance. A train whistled nearby. Lucky snapped awake. She'd been dreaming. Lucky slowly got her bearings and then—

Oh no!

They'd slept through the train arriving!

Lucky realized that Spirit was gone. She ran up to the overhang and looked out at the Water Depot.

"Hendricks, you seein' what I'm seeing?" Horseshoe

said. "I can't believe it." The men had their lassos around Spirit. They tugged on the ropes with force.

"Ha, well, what do you know? This must be my lucky day," Hendricks said with a laugh. He rubbed a hoof-shaped bruise on his face. "Thanks for the new tattoo. Now I have to return the favor."

Lucky ran back to camp. "Abigail! Pru! Wake up. They got Spirit." She shook them. Abigail pulled a marshmallow off her face and ate it. Not waiting for them to rouse themselves, Lucky took off on foot in Spirit's direction.

Abigail followed Lucky with her eyes. "The train! Pru, come on, let's go." Pru and Abigail threw the saddles on their horses and raced after Lucky.

One of the wranglers started filling the train's water tank. Hendricks and the rest of his men pulled on the ropes, forcing Spirit up the train ramp. "Aw, you just couldn't stay away. You wanted to come back to daddy. Get him on the train. Load him up! Yah! Yah!"

"Stop!" Lucky yelled, but she was too far away, and the train and horses were too loud. She ran and ran. "Don't touch him. Don't get in there, Spirit, please."

Pru and Abigail gained on her. "Come on, Lucky," Abigail said.

"Two-hand pickup!" Pru said. The girls reached out

their hands. Lucky remembered the move. She grabbed each hand, and they swung her onto Boomerang's back behind Abigail. Lucky looked over Abigail's shoulder. She could see a lot more from this height. Hendricks pulled out his whip and cracked it on Spirit's neck, forcing him the rest of the way up the ramp and into the train car. Once Spirit was inside, Hendricks slammed the door shut. Chica Linda and Boomerang continued at full speed as the train began to move. Lucky could hear Spirit slamming into the side of the train car, trying to break out, but it was no use.

"Hurry!" Lucky cried. "Get a bit closer; I can jump." Pru shook her head. Boomerang and Chica Linda ran faster, but they were losing this race. The train gradually left them behind and disappeared from sight.

Lucky slid off Boomerang and fell on her knees. "*Nooo!* Spirit!" she yelled after the train. She looked down into her reflection in a small puddle of water. Abigail and Pru slipped off their horses and tentatively moved closer to her.

"You know, once I was playing checkers and I lost all of my pieces—all of my pieces—and I *still* won the game!" Abigail said.

"Um. I think what Abigail is trying to say is, the Lucky we know would never let anything stop her. Until Spirit gets on that boat, we still have a chance," Pru said. "What do you say, Prescott?"

Lucky got to her feet. The wind blew through her hair and she stood as tall as she could. She heard a train whistle in the distance. The other train line was running. Prescotts knew trains.

CHAPTER 11

Pru, Abigail, and Lucky looked on from behind the hill, where they were well hidden. The wranglers were unloading the herd from the train and loading them onto a boat anchored at the dock. Hendricks looked over his shoulder, as if expecting an ambush. "Let's hurry up and get outta here," he said to his men.

"Load 'em up!" Horseshoe said.

"I don't know about you, but I can't wait till I feel that cold hard cash in my hand," Walrus said.

"Mr. Hendricks, Captain says he's ready to go," said a young man in a sailor suit.

"Where is Spirit?" Lucky whispered to Pru and Abigail.

"He's still in the green car!" Pru said. The green train car

115

shook in the distance as Spirit kicked and thrashed. He banged against the door.

"Jeez! What do they have in there?" the young man in the sailor suit asked. "A rhinoceros?"

"What's a rhino-zeros?" Handlebar said. A couple of the wranglers surrounded the green car, getting ready to load Spirit onto the ship next.

"It's now or never," Lucky said. The girls rode toward the caboose of the train. Lucky stood on Boomerang's back and waited for the perfect moment. "Okay, steady." She leapt onto the caboose. "Cover me."

"Chica Linda, let's go! Coming though," Pru said.

"Go, Boomerang, go!" Abigail whooped.

The two girls jumped from around the caboose. Meanwhile, Lucky ran across the tops of the train cars until she reached the green one. She found the top hatch on the car and swung it open. "There you are. Hey, bud!" She smiled at Spirit.

A moment later, the doors to Spirit's car flew open. Handlebar and Horseshoe dove out of the way to avoid them, and Lucky jumped on Spirit's back. "Yah! Yah!" Lucky and Spirit bolted out like the stars of the show. They rode toward the ship, knocking the men aside.

Hendricks shook his head. "Doesn't that girl ever give up? Get rid of her. Hurry up, birdbrains!" Hendricks said to the men remaining on the dock below. Pru and Abigail caught up to Lucky, keeping the wranglers off her.

They were almost there. The plank rose and the ship blew its horn. It began to move away from the dock. Lucky and Spirit skidded to a halt at the dock's edge. Spirit whinnied. The ship was just out of reach. The herd stared helplessly back at them.

"*Noooooo!*" Lucky yelled.

"Ah, would you look at that. Breaks my heart, you comin' so far for nothin'. Kinda brings a tear to my eye," Hendricks said. He made a show of counting his money right there on the deck, flipping through the paper bills. He laughed. "That's a lotta money. *Woo-ooo.*"

Lucky scanned the dock. She spotted a crane platform at the end of the port and several crates stacked together leading up to it. She nudged Spirit with the heel of her red boot. They sprinted around the cargo crates like an obstacle course. No one was paying enough attention to her to notice.

"Hold it right there," one of the dockworkers said. Lucky looked, but he was not talking to her.

"Yes, sir," Pru said to the dockworker, right before pivoting in the opposite direction.

Handlebar, who had been left behind, chased after her on his horse, lasso at the ready. Pru pulled Chica Linda to a halt, and Handlebar's horse stopped dead in its tracks, sending him flying off its back. Horseshoe rode up and tried to lasso Abigail and Boomerang. Abigail and Boomerang ran circles around Horseshoe, roping him instead.

"Oh no, you don't! My six-year-old brother runs faster than you," Abigail said. She jumped off Boomerang and pulled Handlebar to the ground. She hog-tied him, adding even more knots as he struggled to get loose.

Pru followed Abigail's lead. She backed Chica Linda into a couple of dockworkers. They retreated. *Splash!* Into the water. "Nice night for a swim," Pru said.

"They smell better now, too." Abigail chuckled.

Pru nodded. Her eyes searched for Lucky and Spirit.

Lucky and Spirit reached the steep stairs leading up to the crane platform. They began to scale the crates in the same way they had climbed the side of the canyon. Lucky knew not to look down, but she couldn't help it. But she did not see the drop. She saw her friends. She saw the herd. She saw Hendricks and the rest of his men on the ship. All eyes were on her.

"What is she doing? *Ooh*, she's crazy!" Horseshoe said. He freed himself and Handlebar.

"Nuttier than a road apple," Hendricks muttered.

Lucky continued to climb toward the top of the platform. Pru and Abigail watched in horror.

"Is she thinking what I think she's thinking?" Pru shook her head.

"I think so," Abigail said.

"All right, you ready?" Lucky said to Spirit as they reached the platform. Spirit whinnied. A train whistle blew nearby. Lucky glanced in its direction.

A gleaming black steam engine with MILAGRO painted on its side in fresh gold letters sped toward the train station next to the dock. Jim, Aunt Cora, and Al Granger all leaned out the windows in time to see Lucky step onto the platform. Aunt Cora gasped. The train came to a full stop. They deboarded and hurried toward Lucky.

"Lucky!" Jim yelled.

"Fortuna Esperanza Navarro Prescott!" Aunt Cora covered her mouth in shock.

"Oh, that's not good," Al said.

Abigail covered her eyes with both her hands. "Oh, I can't look!" she said, but still peeked between her fingers.

Lucky tuned out the noise. It was now or never. She tapped Spirit's side with her red boot. "Hee-yah!" she said.

Spirit galloped down the length of the platform, gaining incredible speed. Lucky let her body relax. She and Spirit were like one now. They reached the edge of the platform and Spirit leapt into the air. Everything seemed to move in slow motion as they glided through the sky.

All eyes were still on Lucky and Spirit.

Hendricks and his men looked on with shock as she flew toward them.

Pru and Abigail's jaws dropped.

Jim, Aunt Cora, and Al held their breath. But there was also something in Jim's eyes, something like awe. Lucky had never resembled her mother more.

Lucky and Spirit cleared the ship's railing by a nose hair. They landed on the deck. Abigail hugged Pru and they whooped with happiness.

"She made it! She really made it! You think she'd teach me how to do that?" Pru marveled.

"I told you she was fun!" Abigail nudged Pru.

Jim, Aunt Cora, and Al exhaled with relief. Al ran to find Abigail and Pru. Jim and Aunt Cora raced to the edge of the dock. The ship continued to drift into the water.

"Cora, I hope you packed your bathing costume," Jim said. He jumped into the water with a splash.

Aunt Cora, meanwhile, spotted a small rowboat next to the dock. She pushed it into the water.

"Come on, let's get her," Hendricks yelled.

He and his men ran up the stairs of the ship, toward the bow, where Lucky had landed. When they arrived, Spirit was there, but there was no Lucky to be found. The wranglers inched toward Spirit, lassos drawn.

"One of you find the girl. Find her!" Hendricks growled.

Chaos broke out as the men stumbled over one another to figure out who would look for Lucky. Lucky took the opportunity to run out the backside of the lower deck, toward the holding tank where the herd was locked up. She pulled on the bars of the gate, but it would not budge. She looked up at Spirit.

"All right, devil horse. Nice and easy. Yeah . . . I'm gonna teach you some manners," Hendricks said to him. He swung the lasso. "Yah!" Ropes swung from all directions. One of them looped around Spirit's neck. The men grabbed on. "Ha! You're not goin' anywhere."

They cinched the rope. Spirit pulled twice as hard, yanking them forward. He kicked at them with his hind legs and sent Walrus rocketing into the ship's bell. *Ding!* Round 1.

The herd neighed from the lower decks. Spirit charged again. He tossed Chevron head over heels into the bell. *Diiiing.* Round 2.

The herd neighed again.

Walrus got himself up. He grabbed hold of the rope. Spirit spun in a circle and flung him right back into the bell. *Ding.* Round 3.

The young sailor who had been helping them let go of the rope. "I don't get paid enough for this!" he said. He backed away slowly, grabbed a life preserver, and jumped overboard with a splash.

Spirit turned, surprised to find the lasso still on him and

Hendricks still wrenching the rope around the bell pole. "Time to tango. Nice and easy. You're not going anywhere, boy." He pulled the rope tighter. Spirit bucked.

Lucky pushed the rusty lever with all her weight. A wet Horseshoe appeared from around the corner with a pipe in his hands.

"Looking for something?" he said. He approached Lucky, and a hoof kicked through the bars, knocking him out. The pipe rolled from his hands.

Lucky scurried over and picked up the pipe. The mama horse huffed, showing Lucky her big, happy white teeth through the gate. "Atta girl," Lucky said. She used the pipe as leverage to get the gate open. The lever gave! The gate slid open, and the herd stormed from the holding cell.

Lucky quickly ran to the upper deck to help Spirit. The rope tightened around his neck the more he struggled. He was going to strangle himself. "Stop. Stop!" she cried.

Hendricks side-eyed her, sweat beading on his face. "Why you gotta be such a pest?" he said.

Lucky tried to calm Spirit down so he would stop pulling on the rope. "Spirit. Easy, boy...easy. I'm here, boy," she cooed. Hendricks laughed.

"You swim along home now, girl," he dismissed her.

"You first," she said. She vaulted onto Spirit's back. "Hee-ya!"

"No, no, no, wait! Wait," Hendricks said. He backed away. He threw his leg over the deck rail. They didn't wait. They charged. "*Whoaaaa!*" he cried as they rammed him over the rail. He went down and into the water with a big splash.

The whinnying from the herd on the lower deck grew louder. It was as if they were cheering. Lucky threw the lasso off Spirit's neck and they headed toward the other horses. The night had somehow snuck up on them. Horseshoe scurried to the edge of the ship, opened the railing, and threw himself into the water, leaving the railing open. Spirit's eyes widened when he saw the water below. The herd behind them picked up on his nervous energy and inched away. Lucky looked down, trying to refocus her eyes in the growing dark. It was a big jump into rippling black waters that seemed to go on forever. "Easy now, Spirit. It's all right, boy. Trust me." Spirit narrowed his eyes. He stepped forward again.

"Cora, keep rowing. Keep rowing. Lucky! Lucky, no!" Lucky heard Jim in the distance. He was now in the rowboat with Aunt Cora.

"Lucky! We're over here!" Aunt Cora yelled. They were very close now. Aunt Cora raised her arm and shot a flare into the sky.

The night sky lit up as Spirit and Lucky soared into the water. The herd followed.

"Oh no!" Aunt Cora cried.

Lucky broke the surface. Her head went under. She was no longer on top of Spirit. All around her there was a jumble of horse legs paddling to stay up. She tried to figure out which way was up, but she couldn't hold her breath anymore. She heard Jim and Aunt Cora calling her name as her lungs cried out for air. She fought the ocean that was trying to swallow her whole. But finally, thankfully, she came up above water, coughing. Lucky looked all around for Spirit, mindful of the wranglers that might still be in the water.

"Spirit! Where are you?" she said.

Spirit's head popped above the surface nearby. A cry echoed. They turned toward the deck of the ship. Little Brave One and his mama horse were still up there. The mama horse nudged Little Brave One forward. "Quick, grab 'em," said Walrus, who had pulled himself from the bell. The ship was leaving, with or without them.

At the sight of Spirit, Little Brave One jumped into the water, followed by his mama.

Lucky started coughing again. The currents pulled her under. Jim dove and pulled her back up. He struggled to hold her up. "I got you, Lucky. I won't let you go," Jim said. Spirit paddled toward Jim and Lucky. He pulled them both toward the dock, followed by the herd and Aunt Cora in the rowboat.

CHAPTER 12

Abigail and Pru galloped past the docks in the direction of the shore. A pair of lassos whipped out. They hooked Chica Linda and Boomerang.

"Where do you think you're going?" one of the dockworkers bellowed. A whole group of them inched toward the girls. Suddenly, a barrel flew out and smashed the dockworkers out of the way.

"Heads up, boys!" a voice said. Al Granger stepped out from behind a stack of crates, dusting off his hands.

"Dad!" Pru said. Her face wore a number of emotions: surprise, extreme happiness, relief, and guilt. "Oh, Dad. I'm grounded, aren't I?"

"Uh-oh. Nice knowin' ya," Abigail muttered, pulling the ropes off.

Al ran up to Pru and hugged her, taking in Abigail, too. "Yep. For life," he said.

Abigail, Pru, and Al cheered as Lucky and Jim crawled onto shore with Aunt Cora, Spirit, and the rest of the herd.

The water behind them bubbled like an angry sea creature. Hendricks's angry face emerged from the water, too. He lumbered to shore, fists clenched, heading directly in Lucky and Spirit's direction. "Some Lucky's luck just ran out!"

"Yes, yours!" Aunt Cora said. She jumped from the row-boat and *smacked* him hard with her oar.

Lucky had never in her wildest dreams imagined Aunt Cora rowing boats, shooting flares, and fighting bad guys. She was impressed.

But Aunt Cora had only managed to make Hendricks angrier. He licked the inside of his mouth and spit out a tooth. He trudged toward Aunt Cora now.

A lasso landed around Hendricks. Abigail tossed the other end to Lucky. Lucky threw it around Spirit's neck. "Go!" she said. Spirit jolted forward, knocking Hendricks facedown on the sand.

"Let—let me go!" Hendricks growled.

Abigail ran toward him and hog-tied him. She laced

126

the rope over his mouth to shut him up. His men began to crawl onto shore. One by one, Aunt Cora took the oar and smacked them down—a little harder each time.

"Nice rowing, Cora. Woo!" Al laughed. "You got quite an arm."

"Lucky," Jim said. He stared at her, as if seeing her for the first time.

"I know. I broke the rules. Your *one* rule. I'm sorry," Lucky said. "I just wanted to help Spirit. They took his herd. I never meant for it to go like this. We still have to get them somewhere safe."

"No. I'm sorry for everything. I'm proud of you," Jim said.

"Thanks...Dad." Lucky turned to Jim and hugged him for the first time. Tears welled in her eyes. Aunt Cora was crying already. She walked up and wrapped her arms around them both.

"Now go finish what you started. You're a Prescott, and Prescotts never give up," Jim said. He boosted Lucky back onto Spirit's back. Spirit neighed. Jim patted him gently on the face. "You take good care of her," he said to Spirit.

Jim propped up the hog-tied Hendricks. "Kids these days. They grow up so fast," he said. Hendricks groaned.

Pru and Abigail rode up behind Lucky.

"Ready?" Lucky said to the girls.

"Yes," Abigail said.

Pru looked at her map one last time and put it back in her bag. "Come on, Chica Linda!" she said.

"Be back for dinner tomorrow. And no ridiculously dangerous shortcuts," Al said. Pru nodded.

"Let's ride," Lucky said. "Yah! Yah!"

Spirit reared up, calling to the herd. They whinnied in return. The girls set off with the wild horses close behind. Jim, Aunt Cora, and Al waved them off.

"Be careful out there," Aunt Cora called.

Lucky felt utterly free with the wind at her back. She looked at Pru and Abigail. What she felt was beyond words. She finally had friends for life. They left the dock behind and galloped into the woods ahead. Lucky ducked under a branch just in time.

"Whoa! I almost died!" She laughed.

"Eyes on the road, Lucky," Pru said. She was smiling, too.

They rode under the moonlight and came upon a fallen tree. They easily jumped over it. Every hurdle seemed small in comparison to what they'd just been through. The sun was inching back into the sky now. Spirit glanced back every once in a while to check on the herd. He led them through the lush beauty of the wilderness. It was all flora and fauna—no other people as far as the eye could see. He eventually halted; the path had ended. His hooves pranced on the sand. The ocean lay on one side and more forest lay on the other.

"Wow, look at this place!" Abigail said.

Pru glanced at her map for a minute. "This is it. Nothing but wilderness for miles," she said.

Lucky took it all in. She felt overwhelmed, both by the stunning beauty of this place and what it meant to have arrived. She guided Spirit forward, just the two of them. "Well, Spirit. I guess it's time for me to go," she said. He had given her so much in the few days she'd known him. She couldn't be selfish. She looked back at the other horses. "Your herd needs you." She slid off his back. She took a deep breath, fighting back tears. She slowly turned and returned to Abigail and Pru.

Hooves clip-clopped behind her. There was a nudge on her back. She turned around, looking into Spirit's eyes. She could see everything he was feeling. He seemed to be telling her not to go. He pranced, inviting her on more adventures together. Lucky hated disappointing him, but she knew what she had to do.

"I'm sorry, boy, but I can't go with you. My herd needs me, too."

Spirit seemed to understand now. He stepped toward her. She threw her arms around his neck. She lay her face against his and hugged him one last time. Then she took a step back to let go of him. Something else nudged her leg this time. Lucky looked down. Little Brave One nuzzled up against her. Lucky smiled, and bent down so that they were eye to eye.

"Stay wild, brave one," she said to him. She kissed the top of his head, and the foal pranced back to his mama. The mama horse gave Lucky one last nudge, as if thanking her.

"Bye, mama. Take care of the little one," Abigail said, from behind them.

Spirit whinnied, pulling the herd's attention. He reared up on his hind legs and struck out with his front hooves. He landed on all fours, turned back toward the forest, and ran. The herd followed. They picked up speed as they reached the trees.

Lucky watched them disappear into the forest. Mission accomplished. A single tear rolled down her cheek.

CHAPTER 13

The leaves on the trees were turning
gold and orange. Lucky sat on the window ledge while Aunt
Cora bustled around the attic packing up Lucky's things and
once again reliving the day Lucky, Pru, and Abigail saved
Spirit's herd.

"...And then Al came in and said, 'The girls are gone.
They're headed over to Heck Mountain to save a herd of
wild horses. Snips heard them. And rustlers stole your train.'
Then he held out a wanted poster with that...that Hen-
dricks man. I didn't even know what Heck Mountain was.
Then Jim said, 'Why are we standing around here talking?'
Then we all ran outside after him, and Al said, 'We can't
catch them on horseback. Those rustlers have your train.'

131

Jim stopped midway to the barn. He turned to Al, like some, like—'I *am* the train,' he said. Then he pulled the barn doors open, revealing that gleaming black steam engine named after your mother. Then Jim said, 'She's the fastest train ever built. I had some spare parts.' Then he ran his hands along her and whispered, 'Let's go get our girl.' *Oh Jim, Jim, Jim,* I thought! I mean, we'd noticed you were gone before Al told us, but I just figured you were blowing off steam after that last argument." She looked over at Lucky, noticing that she wasn't listening, and softened. "I told you summer would be over before you knew it," she said gently.

Lucky looked down at her PALs bracelet. She picked up her strawberry toy and packed it in the suitcase. Aunt Cora paused, taking note.

"We'll come to visit more. At the holidays. And next summer. And there's still the big festival tonight. Your father is probably wondering what is taking us so long," she said, trying to come up with ways to cheer Lucky up. But she was having trouble smiling herself. Cora looked just as disappointed as Lucky now. Lucky nodded glumly.

"Now, which one of these says Miradero Festival?" Aunt Cora held up two of Lucky's city dresses.

"Uh." Lucky shrugged.

"*Hmm.* I see your point." Aunt Cora turned to Milagro's closet and spotted a red dress hanging there. Her eyes lit up.

The festival was alive with a ranchera singer on the stage, kids eating ice cream, jugglers, and carnival games.

"Oh, Lucky, this dress was the perfect choice," Aunt Cora said, mooning over Lucky in her mother's dress.

Lucky picked up one of the ruffles and nervously wrung the colorful ribbon on the hem. "Thanks, Aunt Cora," she said.

Someone grabbed Aunt Cora's hand. She turned around. "May I offer you a hand there, señorita?" a cowboy said with a flirtatious smile. It was the same cowboy from their first day in Miradero. Aunt Cora turned red. She dabbed her eyes with her handkerchief. As soon as she put the hand-kerchief away, the cowboy took her in his arms and dipped her.

"Well, I never!" Aunt Cora cried, but she was giggling like a schoolgirl.

"Care to make an exception?" he said.

"*Oooh.*" Aunt Cora smiled.

Lucky walked ahead, looking for Jim. Pru and Al Granger cut past her, trying to line dance. "It's step . . . step . . . clap," Pru said to him.

"I think my horse is a better dancer. Step . . . step . . . clap," Al said. "Check me out! Golden-Feet Granger!"

"Not bad for an old man," Pru teased. "I think *my* horse is a better dancer, though."

"But can your horse do this?" Al shimmied.

Pru giggled and rolled her eyes at Lucky as they danced past her. Lucky was laughing now, too. She stopped to listen to a familiar tune coming from the stage behind her. She scanned the crowd, still searching for Jim.

"This next song is for my daughter, Lucky," Jim said. Lucky turned around. He was onstage.

"What?" She said.

"And if *I'm* lucky, one day she'll call this place home."

Lucky made her way through the crowd, until she was standing right in front of the stage. "I *am* home!" she said.

Jim cracked a wide smile, appreciating her answer and her mother's red dress. He timidly began to sing the song that Lucky had come to think of as Milagro's song. But... maybe Lucky'd had it wrong. Maybe it was Jim's song.

Aunt Cora joined Lucky next to the stage.

Lucky locked eyes with Jim. His voice grew, letting go and letting the song say all the things he couldn't.

"Boy, Lucky's dad is bad at singing. Take me closer," Snips said from on top of Abigail's shoulders. Abigail rolled her eyes and moved closer to the stage.

The ground shook. Lucky looked back. Valentina and

Las Caballeras de Miradero circled the crowd. The horses stomped their feet along with the song.

"Wow." Lucky beamed as Jim finished.

Las Caballeras pulled their circle closer on the floor beneath the stage so that Lucky stood in the center; they assumed the same pose from her mother's poster. Lucky looked at them with awe. It was like being in Milagro's zoetrope, like being hugged by her mother. Abigail and Pru ran to the center of the floor to join her.

"Hey, Prescott!" Pru said.

"You're staying?" Abigail nudged.

"Yeah," Lucky said.

"Woohoo! Lucky," Pru and Abigail cheered. They danced and jumped in celebration, as the ranchera singer took the stage again. Fortuna Esperanza Navarro Prescott felt so utterly lucky. She paused and looked off into the distance for a minute. She imagined Spirit and his herd running free in the wilderness.

CLAUDIA GUADALUPE MARTÍNEZ

grew up in the Southwest, dreaming about horses and watching subtitled westerns with her father. She is the author of *The Smell of Old Lady Perfume*, *Pig Park*, and *Not a Bean*. She is also a two-time winner of the Texas Institute of Letters Best Young Adult Book Award, and her work has earned her a Paterson Prize for Books for Young People, an Américas Award Commendation, and a Library Guild Award.